BOOKS BY A~~DAM COLE~~

FICTION

HOFSTADTER'S GRANDCHILDREN

SEVEN WAYS THE WORLD CAN END

Queensland Cycle

THE MYTH OF MAGIC

THE CHILDBEARER

THE PRISON SPELL

Vie A Lyn Series

Book 1 – THE GIRL WITH THE BOW

Book 2 - THE BLUE WOMAN AND THE HIGH WOOD

Mara Solomon, Music Detective

A NOTE BEFORE DYING

THE WHISPER ROOM

NONFICTION

SOLFEGE TOWN

BALLET MUSIC FOR THE DANCE ACCOMPANIST

FIRST LESSONS IN READING MUSIC - THE ONLY PIANO PRIMER YOU'LL EVER NEED

BLUES IMPROVISATION FOR BEGINNERS...AND PIANO TEACHERS

AUTHENTIC WAYS OF TEACHING JAZZ

Visit www.acole.net to see a complete list of available titles!

MOTHERLESS CHILD

MOTHERLESS
CHILD

Adam Cole

http://www.acole.net

Many thanks to my test readers,
of many editions over many years.

This book is dedicated to my sister,
who told me I could do better.

Table of Contents

Part One - What Happened to Basil

November, 2071 - Atlanta Hub, CUSA

In the America that Basil lived in you had to wait a long time for a train. But here, standing on the shiny north platform at the Peachtree Woods Station, Basil Ortega stuck his face into a holographic envelope and within twenty seconds the sensation-generating AVE that produced it knew him and a train rolled into the station. They had sent him a train reserved for veeps because he had just become one.

In the first week after the thunderstorm season, Basil was called to the headquarters of the Noke corporation. He would be providing drug entertainment at one of their parties. He remained in the AVE's glow for a moment, wondering about the thirty-minute ride that would turn him from an eleven-year old toter into a full-fledged drug-man.

When his Padre had first told him he'd be going to Atlanta Proper, Basil assumed it was to help administer the drugs, not to disseminate them himself. He had been amazed when Padre had told him that he'd be going alone. He had never been to the heart of the Proper, much less inside a big CUSA building. He still wasn't even sure he'd be allowed in; he thought that somehow the embodied city would know who he was and reject him.

Basil stepped forward out of the pool of light, the dust-flecks flying inside it like fish in a fishbowl. Even though it was just a holographic space, it seemed to release him reluctantly, the light-ball in front of him closing like a disappointed pair of lips.

He heard the train doors coming together, and he looked for a seat.

The air in the train was a nice contrast from the searing November heat. Meanwhile, the acceleration was so smooth he hardly noticed the transition to flying towards the City Proper. The ramshackle buildings rocketing by him seemed to be fleeing from the growing mass of golden towers that made up the Proper. Those buildings, lying on the other side of the woods, loomed larger by the minute.

This far out the train was generally empty. It only came to Atlanta's run-down outer neighborhoods to bring Shareholders who were making in-person evaluations of real estate or other consultations in the land of the cricket-eaters. Padre had told Basil that as the train got closer to the Proper it would pick up more veeps, some Uniforms. Would they be surprised to see the eleven-year-old boy riding by himself? Maybe if they saw the canvas bag he carried over his shoulder, the bag of a Padre, they wouldn't think twice about it.

At the back of every seat was a site-based AVE, an Audio-Visual Envelope, which generated commercials all the time. If you had good number—that is, if you were rich—you could buy anything from them you wanted. All you had to do was speak to it or touch the pool of light, and it would respond like a budding flower. But Basil didn't have any number at all yet, and he wouldn't have been allowed to buy something if he had.

"Are you thirsty?"

A drink was hovering right in front of his hand, and if he were to move through the image, he knew the AVE would go crazy trying to sell it to him. He kept his hand still while his thoughts spun backwards to the memory of his Padre's words.

"You're just a servant. As am I. Don't forget your sacred obligation, not to stand in the way of the Body and Blood, or you will receive another beating."

Basil had nodded quietly, even though the sound of Padre's voice was only in his imagination. He had been beaten several times and was generally learning how to avoid it. You did a lot of nodding.

Coasting above the canopy of the forest, the train afforded an unobstructed view of the golden towers of the City Proper, wrapped in a loving network of alternate rail lines sailing high above the sparkling Peachtree Esplanade. They loomed so large now that their shadows darkened the windows. On either side of the empty car the lush green alleys that had been planted full of briars with the bright red berries blurred into a messy brown. Basil opened his drowsy eyes to see a car lying on its side by some abandoned railroad tracks, filled with dirt, purple and yellow flowers sprouting out the windows.

How did it get there? What was it? Honda? Prius? The train ran on the old expressways heading in and out of the city, but the pavement had been wrecked years and years ago and no one could have driven on it. Maybe he'd tell Rosa about it if she looked like she cared.

A few minutes later the train pulled into the massive Five Points Terminal, where it became a local. As he stepped off, hundreds of suit- and skirt-clad Shareholders stepped on. A few gave him an odd stare, this little coffee-colored boy with his hemp shoulder-bag nearly as large as himself. Most just stepped around him, as though he were one of the vacumen gliding around sucking the dust off the pavement.

He didn't mind. He was too young to be in awe of Shareholders, young enough to be able to maintain a slight attitude of indifference. Besides, he had too much to think about. He had to remember the routine.

"We do not encourage the indulgences of the unfaithful. But we are in no position to resist. They know we can arrange them, and we are legally obligated to comply. That is why we take our duties even more seriously with the infidels than we do with our own flock. Who are the six who do not lock the gates?"

"Amphetamine," Basil answered. "Cocaine hydrochloride. Methamphetamine. Methylenedioxy-methamphetamine, methylphenidate, nicotine."

"Who are the three who sleep but do not die?"

"Benzodiazepine, gamma-hydroxybutyrate, methaqualone."

"How is the lion brought to sleep with the lamb?"

"By the—" Basil paused. He could not remember.

He involuntarily winced and huddled inward. He had been hit many times for forgetting that last one. *By the China Girl.* He could not forget it now. The words came to him along with a dull ache every time he moved his shoulder.

Someone had decided to do more than stare at him or ignore him. A squat man in a grey charcoal suit and a matching cap approached him.

"Ortega?" he asked.

Basil nodded.

"I was expecting somebody older."

Basil shrugged. He waited patiently, and finally the man in the suit also shrugged and turned away. Basil followed him along the worn platform and up an escalator. In the stone façade of an ancient building that served as the foundation of the station, two bare-breasted stone women stared down absently, holding laurels up over an old catwalk. Basil watched as the escalator slowly pulled them past the two sentinels. At the top of the line, he was dropped onto a sterling, scrubbed plaza. A glass roof filtered the sunlight into a golden haze filled with bugs.

The man led Basil across the celestial courtyard of Five Points Station to where a private car sat waiting, its door open. Basil climbed into the back and the door shut behind him. Driverless, the car eased into the light midmorning traffic.

Basil had never been to the Proper before and Padre had told him not to be seduced. But it was hard not to look as they glided past one after another of the colonnaded buildings of stone and glass, set off from the street by cultivated lawns with bright flower gardens and sleek plastic sculptures with brand names. Exterminators were everywhere, spraying to keep the endless bugs in check. A holographic band played commercials from a bandstand by a statue of someone named Talmadge. Basil's own world seemed drab by comparison; even the interior of the Church, which was beautiful and always clean, seemed ordinary in his memory. Everything here was *new*. Even the bugs in the air sparkled.

An immaculate woman, her skin glowing like a copper plate in the sun, led her two children and a perfectly groomed chow westward, balancing in her high heels on the marble sidewalk. Across the lush expanse of Centennial Olympic Park, happy *pequeños* could be seen screaming with delight as they romped naked in the light fountains.

The car continued down Maynard Jackson for about ten minutes and then slowed at the base of a large pyramid. Before it floated a holographic sign that read *NokeCUSA LLP* in ornate Spanish letters. The car swung around in a smooth "u" until it was parallel to the walkway neatly sheltered beneath the pyramid's base.

Basil got out, clutching his bag close to his side. The man was standing there. Basil had no idea how he had gotten to the pyramid first. Had he run behind the car?

He followed his guide through a revolving door and into a plush, spacious lobby bustling with prim, suited workers. They were lined up in rows before AVEs that sang the promise of various nutrition-bowls and beverages. "Oooo, yes...*I never had anything like it before, Lotta. Are you thirsty?*"

Again, Basil noticed the perfectly manicured air of the place, filtered and cool, nothing like the stifling, close drug-church with its sweet-smelling smoke. An elevator shaft shot diagonally up the spine of the pyramid into the undersides of the office-homes that took up the bulk of the building's mass. Bypassing the curious receptionists with a sly nod, the man took Basil across the lobby where a lift was waiting patiently for them. As they ascended Basil watched the floors collapsing beneath him, stacking like a deck of cards. For a moment, the elevator was enveloped by darkness as it moved towards the top floor.

An electric pulse seemed to eat the man alive, traveling diagonally down his body until he was gone from sight. Before he had completely vanished, his head blinked and the body reappeared. Now Basil understood. This was a holographic projection. The man was here to make sure Basil didn't get lost, but he wasn't *here.*

"Where do you live?" Basil asked him.

"In a coffin at the Marriott Marquis," the man replied, twiddling his thumbs. "You ever been Proper?"

Basil shook his head. The man, who did not see the gesture, looked down and said, "Eh?"

"No," Basil said.

"It's pretty, isn't it?"

"Where do you live?" the man wanted to know.

"Sandy Springs."

"You really have drugs in that bag?"

Basil nodded.

"Anybody ever try and take that bag from you before?"

Basil had never considered that possibility. As far as he knew, no one had ever stolen from a Padre in sight of an AVE. Uniforms would arrive to arrest anyone stupid enough to attempt it. Of course, he wasn't a real Padre. He folded his hands and looked away.

When the elevator finally hit top, the man took Basil up a short escalator. Now he could see the uppermost expanse of offices, the desks of the secretaries laid out like watch posts in front of the huge mirrored glass doors and walls of the veeps. All the voices combined and floated up to the blue sky which seemed to be trapped in the pyramid's ceiling-point.

"Wait here, okay?" the man said to Basil.

He went on to one of the desks and exchanged words with the secretary behind it. She directed him with a transparent-nailed finger to a spiral crystal staircase a little way off. The man nodded, turned around, and walked back to Basil.

"You sit here, *capitán.* He'll call you up when he's ready to see you. Dow!" With a cordial wave, the man bowed and was gone.

The secretary, who was talking simultaneously to three holographic heads that floated in various places around her, did not seem to notice Basil. He sat down in a nearby chair. It molded to fit his bottom. Then it began to vibrate a little.

"They don't believe. They have no souls."

"No one can quit but them."

"Little boy?" the secretary called down, standing over him. Basil had fallen asleep in the vibrating, form-fitting chair. Basil blinked, dazed. As if on cue, the chair ceased to shake. "You can go up." The secretary watched Basil get to his feet. He clutched his bag and plodded to the crystal stair.

Mr. Sattari's name was holographically projected on a door that dematerialized as Basil came within a foot of it. It was the only executive door in the entire upper chamber that did not mirror the person approaching it. Instead it was opaque, black. Once the door had vanished, Basil could see that Mr. Sattari's office had two stories. Little boats floated in a small pool in the far-left corner—real boats, real water, no holograph. Along the other corner sat what looked like a wide, squat armoire, its handleless doors closed tight at the bottom, its one drawer lying open in the middle, displaying a long row of black and white blocks arranged in a regular pattern of twos and threes. Leather-bound books, their spines decked in stately purples and forest greens, lined glass-enclosed shelves. Certain sections of the floor were transparent and revealed several stories below.

Three servants fluttered about the space. A woman in a purple corset that pressed her breasts up was removing the remains of a food tray to a hole in the back wall. Two barelegged men in tunics were busily dusting with an ion-sweeper.

Mr. Sattari's desk was on the upper level, which was accessible only by a short arching stairway of wide platforms that seemed to have no visible supports. The high plateau was crowded by a huge mahogany desk; a straight-backed chair facing it; a more comfortable chair behind it, in which Mr. Sattari sat; and a small sofa off to the side whose back was unprotected from the one-story drop. Just behind Sattari's left elbow, an unmoving servant with a solemn expression stood at the ready for anything he might desire, though whether the servant was real or holo Basil couldn't tell.

Mr. Sattari, the *Siyo* of the Noke Corporation, had a stern face which was frozen deep in concentration in the light of his AVE. His fingers manipulated symbols which floated around his head in a green halo, his eyes oblivious to the images blinking in the air before him as if he could see their characteristics without regarding them. To his right was a small wooden bowl full of shelled almonds.

Basil should have been in awe of this man with his green halo of faces and data. The *Siyo* of the Noke Company controlled one of the many conglomerates that made up the Corporation of the United States of America.

But Basil had his own job to do. His position in the Drug Church kept him from losing himself. The *Siyo* would need him.

As Basil ascended the platforms, he had the strange sensation of getting smaller. Mr. Sattari's expression did not change; his brow did not unfurrow, nor did his eyes lose their focus. By the time Basil had mounted the lip of the last stair, the *Siyo* had returned his gaze to his fingers.

Basil stood uncomfortably for a second. "Sit down," Mr. Sattari dictated in a faraway voice. Basil took the straight-backed chair and waited.

After a while, Mr. Sattari looked up with the same distant expression and said, "I was expecting the Padre."

"He sent me, Mr. Sattari." Basil used his best Spanish.

Mr. Sattari regarded the boy critically up and down. "You're very young."

"I know the rites," Basil said, defending himself. "He sent me on my first assignment because I know them all."

Still, Mr. Sattari regarded him severely. "How old are you?"

"That doesn't matter, *señor*," Basil answered.

Surprised, Mr. Sattari started back in his chair. His eyebrows had exploded upwards, but his eyes remained where they were. Then he nodded, relaxed, sat forward. "You're right. You have the drugs, after all, don't you?" Now that Basil was closer, the *Siyo* looked very different. His brown face appeared much older, despite the absence of any grey in the bob of jet-black hair. He sat stiffly, his body thin and erect under a white suit-blouse tied with a black ribbon at the neck.

"The Body and Blood," Basil corrected.

Mr. Sattari barely heard him. He leaned back in his chair and regarded Basil more curiously. "How old are you?" he asked again, but this time the meaning of the question was different.

"Eleven years."

"So young."

"Most boys start learning at four."

"Do all eleven-year-olds make these trips?"

"My Padre's a stern man," said Basil with curious emphasis.

"So you really know what you're doing," Mr. Sattari answered, understanding his meaning.

Basil nodded.

"What about your mother?"

"Don't have a mother," Basil answered. "She moved to another Church."

"Really?" asked the *Siyo*. "That's something we have something in common. I didn't have a mother either. I sometimes think I can remember her. Not her face, but everything else." The *Siyo* passed his hand in front of his face. "Maybe she was there when I was a little child. I can almost see her in my mind, but then she backs out...fades away. Sometimes I feel her. She must have held me..." Mr. Sattari paused, his eyes distant again, no longer talking to the boy. Basil didn't reply. He had heard that sometimes before drug-parties the clients felt like sharing personal things, that the experience of taking the drugs scared them, and they wanted to confess before they said things they shouldn't.

"You know we're not worshippers," Mr. Sattari said abruptly.

Basil nodded.

"But you bring us the drugs anyway."

"We have to," Basil replied. Immediately he wondered if he should have said so in front of Mr. Sattari's servant, still standing obliquely behind the *Siyo*. Although anyone might have guessed how CUSA and the Drug Church were connected, no one was supposed to say it openly. CUSA liked to pretend that the Church, by offering free, limitless substances to its addicts, was evil. But the Corporation paid for everything. It was a compromise. The Church broke its rules, and the Corporation got its parties.

"It's a strange thing," Mr. Sattari said into his hand.

Basil didn't know what the *Siyo* meant. He sat in the straight-backed chair and waited.

"You give these drugs to addicts for free."

"Yes, *señor*." It was true. The addicts came and the Church provided. No questions were ever asked; no demands were ever made. Whatever means of worship addicts required, they got.

"Why?"

"They come, we serve."

"But they aren't happy," Mr. Sattari argued.

"Not until they use."

"But the drugs make them vomit. They turn them into slaves. They blindly roam CUSA like zombies. They don't even know how to feed themselves."

"We take care of them," Basil replied.

Mr. Sattari paused to consider. "Yes, but—" he began. "Why don't you help them quit?"

"That's their part," Basil said.

"What?"

"That's the burden placed upon them," Basil said, parroting his Padre.

"What do you mean?"

"They have to quit. They take the drugs to learn what they need to learn. When they get enlightenment, they quit."

"But they never quit!" Mr. Sattari exclaimed, obviously irritated. "The drugs are so addictive!"

"It's up to them to quit," Basil said, simply.

Baffled, Mr. Sattari stared through Basil the same way he stared through his green halo. He leaned back, his hand on his mouth, his eyes pensive. After a while he straightened up. "Are you going to give my people addictive drugs?"

"No," Basil said. "We don't give those to nonbelievers."

Mr. Sattari nodded again through his hand. He seemed to have dismissed Basil with a thought. "Well," he said. "That's fine. Why don't you go down and wait by Ms. Sanchez's desk? The party won't start until this evening." By the time Basil had gotten to his feet, Mr. Sattari was lost in his symbols again.

So Basil descended the platform arc and exited into the lobby, feeling the door solidify behind him. He came down the stair to stand in front of the secretary's desk. Ms. Sanchez gestured to the chair in which he had sat before, saying "You can sit there."

Basil slid into the chair again. It molded to fit his form. Then it began to vibrate once more.

"We do not encourage the indulgences of the Infidel..."

"Little boy?" The secretary, Ms. Sanchez, was standing over him and smiling. "It's time."

Basil shook himself. The chair had once again gone still. The sky trapped in the apex of the pyramid was now black. Ms. Sanchez extended her hand. Basil took it and pulled himself out. He looked back at the chair suspiciously.

"Usually clients aren't in there for more than forty-five minutes," she said. "You were in stasis for four hours. You can feel it." She sounded sympathetic. "You don't notice the time passing, but you can feel it." Basil said nothing. She nodded to affirm her own words.

He felt naked, overly light. He looked himself over, and his breath caught in his throat. Trying to keep the trembling out of his voice, he said, "My bag." He was missing his drug-bag, with the sacred implements inside.

"We have it," said the secretary, reassuring him.

"Give it to me." Basil was quickly coming to himself as he looked into her eyes. The secretary frowned, unpleasantly surprised at the tone of his voice. "Give it to me now!"

Put off, she found she could not answer him as she would have spoken to a child. She shook her head a little as she turned. "Follow me. I don't have it." Basil walked right at her heels, ready to overtake her at the moment he saw his property.

"*Oooo...yes...*" came the voice from all directions, soft and sinuous. The AVEs were spaced every twelve meters along the wall, broadcasting at low volume. Voices came from everywhere, selling, accessible to anyone who came within reach of the spherical halo. Basil and the secretary arrived at an open doorway.

Several people were in a bare conference room, sitting around a low table on a sofa and chairs. The canvas bag was lying on the table.

Startling the occupants of the room, Basil sped towards his bag and grabbed it by the strap. They laughed, thinking him the child of an office-worker. "Hey, *amigo*, that's not yours," one of them said, rising.

Basil had gone into the corner with his back against the wall and glared at the man who had begun moving towards him.

"It is," said the secretary quickly. "It is his. This is the dealer."

"Him?" the man asked, pointing at Basil. He didn't seem to believe it.

The secretary nodded. Basil rummaged through his bag. It had been opened, but nothing was missing. He let out a tiny sigh of relief.

"You'll be in here," the secretary said to Basil across the room. "You can start any time someone asks." Basil nodded at her curtly, to let her know he was ready for her to be gone. Making a funny shape with her mouth, the secretary turned on her heel and strode from the room.

The four people who had been sitting when he entered now regarded Basil. The one who was standing stepped towards him. "So, kid," he said. "You're the dealer."

Basil nodded, still holding his bag tight.

"We didn't go in it," he said, pointing at the bag. He was lying, but they were fortunate they hadn't opened anything. People had died at parties by ingesting unidentified powders and drinking liquids meant for syringes. If anyone at this party was hurt, Basil would be held responsible.

"When can we start?" a woman asked him.

"Ms. Sanchez said we could start any time," a man interjected.

"Well, I want to start now," said the other woman in the room, getting to her feet. She moved towards Basil. Coming near him, she slowed awkwardly. Impassive, he watched her approach, but made no move to receive her.

"What do we do?" she asked, uncertain.

She had never taken before. "*White Lamb for the child*," Padre would have said. Basil opened his bag with a slow, practiced movement. He knew what to pull out without having to look. He removed a small pill, flexible like a sponge, with his fingertips.

She reached out her palm, but he shook his head. He signaled for her to get on her knees.

Smoothing her skirt, she knelt before him. As he held the pill before her mouth her eyes went soft. Like a child, she opened her lips, an expression on her face that was part surprise, part exultation, and solemnly he slipped the pill between them. "Don't chew," he instructed. "It has to sit beneath your tongue for thirty seconds. Then swallow it."

She nodded and closed her lips, remaining still. "In the name of the Holy Spirit," Basil said, making the sign of the cross over her. The other people in the room were getting to their feet. The man who had remained standing the whole time quickly knelt next to the woman, whose eyelids had begun to flutter.

"I want a Green Bus. Do you have a Green Bus?" he asked eagerly. "I had one last time." Basil nodded and reached for the capsule.

Next came a small man with wiry arms and weak eyes. He hardly looked at Basil as he knelt on the floor before him. Basil recognized the telltale expression of a Gamer. He was employed to play virtual scenarios in the AVE all day long. Basil knew about Gamers because they had to be blessed differently. Gamers rarely saw the world. Most of them had remained in full-time login since their school-days. Because they already lived in their own little world it was not helpful to give them certain kinds of substances. Basil had been instructed to make their forced sojourn in the physical world tolerable through mood-enhancers. Padre had told him that for Gamers this would suffice.

Just as the first woman was entering her convulsions, several other people came into the office. By the time her movements had stopped and her euphoria began, twenty people were lined up waiting for Basil's benediction.

It was always busiest at first, Padre had told him. The beginners rarely came back for seconds until near the end of the night, and the more experienced knew enough to wait before mixing effects. Those who didn't know how to be careful, Basil would have to turn away for a while.

He had no trouble. By the end of the first hour, he was the only responsible person in the building; the rest of the occupants were engaged in drug-play. When things had finally slowed enough for him to take a break, he stood up, closed his bag, tucked it beneath his arm, and left to roam the top floors of the pyramid.

He had seen the effects of the sacred implements all his life, but only on the faithful, who used the addictive drugs. None of tonight's blessings would induce vomiting or generate hazardous delusions. As he walked around he saw some office workers leaping from table to table in a kind of line-dance, overtipping empty wine-glasses. A few sat in chairs and sofas in solitude and watched their own little mind-shows. Others talked back to the visions. They would not remember what they saw. As he passed the stasis chair he saw the secretary, Ms. Sanchez, sitting in it. She was trapped in an endless vision compounded by the technology of the chair.

Basil had not expected this situation, nor did he know how to handle it. The woman might be in real danger. Putting a hand on her arm, he brought the chair to its still state. She did not blink.

He pulled her gently from the chair by her arms. She came out easily. Laying her on the floor face down, he checked her pulse. It was slow but steady. He pulled a salve out of his pack, wetted two fingers, and applied a patch to the side of her neck. Then he left her. She would soon recover and come back for more.

He wandered past a couple who held each other immobile, their arms wrapped around one another like two mummies in a single coffin. Another pair stood face-to-face just down the hall. They were trying to touch one another but seemed unable to do it. Their fingers and faces came close again and again. Each person seemed perplexed by their absolute inability to connect.

Standing next to them, three men lay inside the AVE and watched the Denver Post at New England Kelloggs game, not really understanding what they were looking at. Instead of cheering, they stared, baffled, at the running men all around them. Basil strolled past, walking through the 3-D image of the players.

Finally, several people accosted him at the bottom of the crystal stair. "We want more," said a man in a black frilled shirt and matching vest. "I want the Rainpowder. Do you have the Rainpowder?"

Basil shook his head.

The man looked cross. These were executives like Mr. Sattari. They were not used to hearing no, especially from someone like him. "I know you have it," he said. "I took it at a party once before. I know you guys keep it in your bags."

Basil shook his head, feeling a little nervous. He didn't want anyone to see him lose his confidence, so he stood still and stared at the wall.

The man's expression darkened. "Give it to me *now*, you shitty little twerp," he said. He grabbed Basil by the lapel with a dark fist.

"Leave him alone," said another man, interfering with his hand on the first man's bicep. "He's just a kid."

"But this other stuff is like candy," argued the accoster. "I want you to try the real thing, and I know he's got it." He glared at Basil. The boy returned the stare, outwardly keeping his calm over the panic that was making him tremble.

"*If you lose control, you've got to go,*" Padre had said. "*Don't let them see you're afraid or they'll take the bag.*" Basil kept control. He kept his gaze fixed on the man who was holding him. "*Remember, he's off balance,*" Padre told him. "*When he's in the clouds, you're smarter and stronger than him.*"

The executive frowned down at Basil. Even in his current state he did not appear as if he would be intimidated by an eleven-year-old. Basil began to be afraid that he'd given the man the wrong dosage or combination.

"Look," said a woman from behind. "He's just a little kid. Take him up to Mr. Sattari. He'll make him give it to you."

The accoster nodded. "You're right," he said. He grabbed Basil firmly by the wrist and began pulling him. The others followed, whooping, excitement surging behind them until, like a wave, they stood before the doorway to Mr. Sattari's subdued, dark office.

One of the men made a tentative gesture at the door. It reluctantly became semi-transparent, as if begrudging him a limited access. An image of Sattari appeared on it. The *Siyo* was still dancing through holograms with his fingers, though the servant had vanished. He did not look up. Basil suddenly realized that Mr. Sattari was the only one who had not yet come to him. The *Siyo* was still attired in his work clothes, still penetrating the light-symbols with his fingertips.

"Mr. Sattari, why are you still workin-*guh?*" an older woman giggled like a child. Mr. Sattari looked up mildly, a patient expression in his eyes.

"Mr. Sattari, you're missing the party!" said the first worker.

"That's all right," he said, smiling a little. "I'll come down later. I'm sure the boy has lots of drugs still." He had not seen Basil.

The boy dealer was pulled out roughly by the disgruntled employee. "Mr. Sattari, he's holding out on us! I asked him for some Rainpowder and he said no. I know he has—"

Upon seeing Basil, Mr. Sattari's expression changed dramatically. The *Siyo* surged to his feet. "Let him go! *Now!*"

Cowed and terrified, the man fell back into the shelter of his group. Everyone had fallen silent. They stood there like guilty children, looking away now, afraid to move.

"Mr. Artui," said the *Siyo*. The man snapped to attention. Mr. Sattari spoke with icy deliberation. "There are twenty-million unemployed people in the Atlanta Hub. You are about to be one of them."

Artui paled and his legs began to buckle. Mr. Sattari glared at him. "You have had enough. Go back to your office and go to bed. I will see you in the morning." Artui hastened to comply and was gone in a heartbeat.

Mr. Sattari swept his grave eyes over the rest of them for a long moment. "Go," he finally told them. "I'll handle our dealer. If any of you lay another *finger* on company property, your contracts will be terminated."

The cowed employees nodded their collective heads in a furtive way, no longer wanting to be seen. Half backing, half tripping, the group of workers made their way down the hall, a couple of them barely restraining a few giggles at last as they fell out of earshot.

Mr. Sattari cocked his finger in the air and the door vanished. Basil could see him now, farther away. The *Siyo* gestured at him to enter and he did.

Mr. Sattari cocked his finger again and the door became extremely solid behind Basil. As Basil ascended the arcing stair, Sattari looked down at him. "I'm sorry," he said. "Did they hurt you?"

Basil shook his head. He was trembling a little, but he felt he had to keep himself under control. A Padre wouldn't show his feelings.

Mr. Sattari sighed heavily and sat back down in his chair. For a while, he lost himself behind his hand, swimming in a wash of thoughts. Then his eyes flitted up to Basil.

"Here," he said, gesturing in the air with his finger. The air lit up where his finger was for a second. Instantly a servant emerged from the wall bearing a huge glass of water, with real ice cubes.

Basil looked at it, stunned. Sattari nodded once, and Basil watched as the servant put it on the table next to him. He had never had Proper Water before, and had never even seen ice cubes except in commercials. When he touched the cold glass, it seemed even more real than he was, and the shock of it on his fingers seemed to revive him somehow.

"Why didn't you give him the Rainpowder? Is that what it was?"

"I'm not allowed," Basil answered quietly, seizing the glass as quickly as he could. The ice slid onto his face as he tilted the glass, and the water was cold in his throat. He relaxed in spite of himself and a little trail escaped to his neck. He wiped it distractedly with one of his long sleeves.

"Do you have it?"

Basil nodded yes. "I'm supposed to carry it in case I meet an addict. But I'm not allowed to give it to you." He paused to consider his response. "It's for the faithful."

Mr. Sattari considered for a moment. Then, as if he had been thinking about it since their earlier conversation that afternoon, he said, "It's the mission of your believers to quit."

"Yes," Basil nodded, drinking the rest in a single go.

"How can they quit when you keep giving them drugs?"

Swallowing, Basil answered, "We support them so they don't have any excuse."

"What?" Mr. Sattari seemed baffled.

"Only they can quit," Basil insisted. Still vexed, Mr. Sattari frowned at Basil. "Padre could explain it to you," Basil said. He was pushing aside the ice with his fingers, trying to get the last drops.

"Wait for the ice to melt," said Mr. Sattari. "What do you mean only they can quit?"

"They take the drugs to see," Basil tried to explain. "We make sure nothing gets in the way."

"What do they see?" Mr. Sattari wondered aloud.

Basil hesitated. "I don't know," he replied. "We're not allowed to take the dru—the Body and the Blood."

"You've never taken them!" Mr. Sattari repeated, astonished. Basil shook his head no. "Why?"

"We're not allowed," Basil repeated. At first, Basil appeared as though he either would not or could not explain. "Sometimes they see demons," he said. He examined his glass carefully. The large beads on the outside resembled huge, frozen water droplets that would not surrender their treasure.

"Demons," Mr. Sattari's voice sounded hoarse, as if the word was heavy on his throat.

"Sometimes they see angels, too," Basil said quickly. "They scream and carry on, or they sit for hours, sometimes days; some of them, they don't eat unless we feed 'em, don't drink unless we give 'em something. They just see and see." He looked hard at the glass, hoping more water would appear so he wouldn't have to ask for it.

"And do they ever quit?" Mr. Sattari asked.

Basil shrugged, putting the glass on Sattari's desk. "Not when they're with us. They come and go, they move from Church to Church. One day, maybe, they stop coming. We never see that part."

"What do you suppose they see that makes them stop coming?" Mr. Sattari asked.

The secretary's face appeared. "*Siyo,*" said the face. "Your wife wants to talk to you, but you've got her blocked. Do you want me to open a link?"

Mr. Sattari hesitated. Basil watched him curiously.

With a sideways jiggle of his head, Mr. Sattari shut his AVE off. The faces babbling around him vanished. Now only Basil and the *Siyo* were in the room.

Shifting, as though the weight of the light had been a huge burden on his head, the *Siyo* leaned sideways and cocked his neck to look at Basil. He seemed to be trying to decide something.

Abruptly, he spoke. "I want to quit Noke," the *Siyo* said.

Basil jumped, quite taken aback by the words and tone of Sattari's voice. "What did you say?"

"You heard me," said the *Siyo*. "I hate this place. I hate what it stands for, and all the people who help it along. Every day I despise myself for doing my job." Mr. Sattari paused to regard Basil's reaction. "Does that surprise you?"

Basil shook his head quickly, emphatically. He thought it best to agree with the *Siyo*.

"I want to see," Mr. Sattari said.

Basil pretended he didn't understand. His eyes fell upon the objects on Mr. Sattari's desk. Holographic projections were organized and stacked upon each other. One of the papers blinked.

"I want to see," Mr. Sattari repeated.

Basil looked up at him as the dealer again. "You want to escape?"

Mr. Sattari's brow wrinkled. "No," he clarified. "I don't want any party drugs. I want to see like the faithful see. I want the real drugs."

"You can't take those," Basil said.

"Why not?"

"You're not a believer."

"I want to believe."

Basil's face wrinkled in consternation. Padre had never spoken to him about this. Nobody joined the Church. Addicts simply appeared, already lost, looking for a fix. Basil wavered. "I don't—"

"You have them with you. You said you did."

Basil began to get nervous. He remembered the locked door behind him.

Mr. Sattari went on. "I have demons I need to see. I have to talk to my demons."

"I can't," Basil said. "I—"

"You must," Mr. Sattari said sternly.

"I don't know how. I'm not a Padre."

"You have them. Just give them to me."

"I can't!"

"Give...them...to...me..." growled Mr. Sattari, standing up again to his full height.

"I can't!" Basil's voice was strained and anxious. Clutching his bag, he retreated from Mr. Sattari. The executive glared, but not directly at Basil.

"You don't understand," Sattari said gruffly, trying to explain to Basil. "It's not sane here. You see? I've decided to become insane so that I can think clearly."

Basil regarded Mr. Sattari carefully from the edge of the platform. The *Siyo* was standing behind his desk looking down at the glass floor, as if reading the words that came out of his mouth on the polished transparent surface.

"I need—" he began. Stopping, he brought his hand to his mouth to consider. "I need absolution...to be released from my responsibility, if only for a minute. I need...*absolution,*" he said again. The *Siyo* looked at Basil now, his questioning eyes soft and pliant like a dog's. "Aren't you supposed to give that?"

Basil nodded. Then he shook his head. He didn't know. "To the faithful," he stammered.

"I want to join," Mr. Sattari said again.

Basil shook his head.

"I said I want to *join!*" Mr. Sattari's palm slammed onto the surface of the desk. The wet ice in the glass collapsed. Virtual documents flew into the air and quickly reorganized themselves in a blinking pattern.

Basil backed up a step, though there was nowhere to run. "You going to hurt me?" he asked.

That stopped the *Siyo*. But it didn't shock him. He seemed to be considering, his face taking on the familiar glassy, distantly rational expression. He lowered himself slowly into his chair once more, moving forward a little. Its springs adjusted with a groan to his weight. It was an old-fashioned chair, not resting on a magnet or an air-cushion. "Do you play your history?" Sattari asked.

Basil paused for a moment before answering. "I play a little."

Mr. Sattari held the boy in his gaze, unblinking. "Have you ever played *The Sword of Hendrix*?"

Basil did not want to say "no" to the *Siyo*. He kept still, returning the stare.

Sattari's eyes lit up. "It's brilliant!" he said. "If you ever really want to understand CUSA, you must play it. Do you log on to school? Do you know who Hendrix was?"

Basil hesitated. Quickly, Sattari spoke up. "He was the man who created the Corporation in order to rescue the old USA from its waste and dissent." Sattari looked away and swallowed. "In the game, you become Hendrix. You are trying to end the Correction. You must make the decisions which will defeat your rivals and satisfy the American People, all the while keeping the Sino Conglomerate from buying us. It's a difficult game. But in facing his demons, you come to recognize his brilliance, the impossible ideas he was able to spin.

"We had to be great again, do you see?" The *Siyo* gazed intently at Basil, trying to ascertain whether the boy could understand. "By seizing all of this country's assets, making all of us employees of one great nation, he saved us!"

Mr. Sattari's eyes looked off to the left. "It's really stirring," he said, "to walk the flooded streets of old Washington. To be there for the Kansas Famines, the Armageddon Assembly, the Sterility Incentive." Mr. Sattari breathed deeply.

He looked back at Basil. "If you're CUSA, you have to make lots of decisions every day. How much to spend, how much to keep, because lots of people are depending on you to stay alive.

"One of the most difficult decisions Hendrix had to make was how to keep the climate steady. We're in a delicate, constant negotiation with the Sino Conglomerate, MexIran, all the corporations of the world. This is how we keep enough water for everyone. Only, there isn't enough water."

"Can't you do something?" Basil wanted to know.

"Only so much," Mr. Sattari said, shaking his head. "Our revenue stream depends on keeping the right amount of people on payroll to keep the economy stable. It's one of my tasks to make sure that we sustain only as many as the environment can stand." Mr. Sattari sat back and made a tight mesh with his fingers to support his neck. "Right now, the economy, the environment, is out of balance. Our actuaries predict irreversible collapse in 26 days."

Basil blinked, unable to conceive of the end of the world. He saw the small pool of water in the glass that had formed around the bottoms of the ice cubes. Then he asked, "What are you going to do?"

"Well!" said Mr. Sattari, releasing his head from his hands with a nod. "We don't know, do we? We have to find a solution or our society falls apart. Then where are we? What do *you* think we should do?"

Basil shrugged. "Stop selling water?"

Mr. Sattari shook his head. "Yes, but how? CUSA relies on a certain amount of revenue from sales of our water to keep the economy stable. If we curb that revenue, we risk sending many, many people into poverty." Mr. Sattari's eyes seemed to cross as he looked away from Basil. "They might rise up again. Become violent. That's not good, is it?"

Again, Basil didn't know how to answer. Shrugging was all he could think of to do.

Sattari ignored the response. "I have to eliminate some of our domestic demand in the right way. Just enough to keep us under the thirst threshold, but not so much that revenues will be disrupted." Mr. Sattari paused. "One million one-hundred-fifty thousand and nine." he finally said.

When Basil showed no sign of understanding, the *Siyo* went on. "We can't simply ask people to stop consuming. That wouldn't be fair. We could terminate their employment, make them poorer, but once those people stop working, they would become even more of a burden on the economy.'" He stopped again. "You know what I'm talking about?"

Basil knew, but he was afraid. If he understood correctly, the *Siyo* was supposed to order a million people to die.

The *Siyo* continued speaking. "Basil, I don't tell these things to just anybody. They're secrets. Do you understand?"

Now Basil nodded because it was what the *Siyo* wanted. His bag seemed heavy on his shoulder. These were secrets he didn't really want to know, and the weight of them scared him.

"You see," said the *Siyo*, "Many of our decisions are automated, controlled by an algorithm and executed by the network. But not this one. The Rand Act prohibits technology from taking life. That must be done by a person, a *Siyo*."

Still going on in that reassuring, fatherly tone, Mr. Sattari continued, "I wanted you to understand what my job is like, why I need absolution."

Basil's throat tightened as he clutched the bag before him. Half the ice in the glass was melted, but Basil didn't dare reach for it to drink. "You see," said Mr. Sattari, "a man like me, he has to make extremely difficult decisions.

For the last time, Mr. Sattari rose solemnly to his feet. "You have to make a difficult decision, too. Right now."

Basil didn't want to hear. He wavered on the edge of the platform, rocking from side to side.

Mr. Sattari put his finger over one floating button near his desk. "This symbol," he said, moving the icon over a little, "begins a process which will solve CUSA's problem. Executives will make adjustments and give orders. Termination centers will open for 24-hour service. Young Guns will come around to peoples' houses and begin taking families away. More than a million of them." The *Siyo* moved his finger. "*This* symbol," he said, "opens the door and lets you out.

"You can stand there and watch while I begin ordering the early removal of someone you know, or you can give me the drugs I want, which will surely incapacitate me and possibly make me forget you. Then you can get out the door and run to your Padre."

Mr. Sattari looked expectantly at him. "Make a choice."

Basil did not answer. His eyes searched the room, the little glass ceiling raised to a point above them, the distant lights of the buildings beyond, the desk, Mr. Sattari's face, Mr. Sattari's fingers.

"I don't want to," said Basil.

"I don't want to either," said Mr. Sattari. "Isn't that awful? We all have to make difficult decisions. You have ten seconds," said Mr. Sattari.

Basil looked at the door, which was obviously locked. He wanted to run, to get out. "One," came the *Siyo's* voice. He looked up at Mr. Sattari, who was watching him with his finger over the first button. What if Mr. Sattari slipped and his finger fell through it? "*Two,*" continued Mr. Sattari. "Three. Four..."

Basil could smell the sweat of the man, now. Mr. Sattari remained still as stains grew around his armpits and his hand hovered over the symbol.

Basil looked through his bag, going over the possible choices. He put his bottom on the floor, his back to the empty space. What would Padre suggest? A stimulant; the *Siyo* would feel it much sooner. He was asking for a hallucinogen, but that would take too long. Basil's hands found a syringe and a phial with a rubber membrane sealing it. He pulled them out. Leaving his bag on the floor, he rose to his feet and held the implements up to Mr. Sattari. "This is what you want," he said.

Mr. Sattari gazed in wonder at the phial and syringe. "That will make me a...believer?" he asked in a surprisingly small voice.

Basil nodded. Mr. Sattari reached for them, but Basil held them back. "Take off your blouse," he instructed.

Immediately Mr. Sattari did so. He fell back into his chair with a thump of flesh against leather. Basil looked at the executive's virgin forearm. The veins were large and clearly defined.

As Basil came around the desk, Mr. Sattari's body lurched forward. Basil jumped back, but Mr. Sattari was only reaching for the symbol that unlocked the door. Falling into his chair again, he looked up at Basil. "I've ordered a rickshaw to drive you to the station," he said. He offered up his soft forearm to Basil.

His heart beating wildly now, Basil applied a tourniquet to Mr. Sattari's triceps. Returning to his bag, Basil took the syringe, expelled the air, and inserted it into the membrane. He drew all the fluid out of the phial.

Smoothly Basil injected the needle into Mr. Sattari's forearm. " 'He was crucified'"—he gave the syringe a slow, steady push—"'under Pontius Pilate, suffered, and died.'" Fascinated, Mr. Sattari watched the fluid leave the syringe and enter his vein. "'And on the third day he rose.'" Now the drug was completely gone and was coursing through Mr. Sattari's system.

The *Siyo* leaped to his feet. An obscene grimace stretched his face so far it could have pulled the skin from the bone. He began to shake triumphantly. "Go," he whispered to Basil.

But Basil was already gone.

Part Two - What Happened to Rosa

Two Aprils Later

It was an old-time bus, stinking of exhaust, the kind that you only ever saw on roads heading out of CUSA. It had some newer parts sticking out around the outsides, and it wasn't that big. It had old blue painted stripes, and the tires were all worn at the letters. Rosa was scared about that until she got on and saw the smelly pile of tires inside at the back.

Fifteen people followed her and her family. First was Firoz, a tall, skinny waste of a man with black half-circles under his bloodshot eyes. He didn't know the ground was there. He didn't have any luggage except for one tiny bag hanging from his shoulder. He boarded, sat in the back corner of the bus, and looked out the window.

The Kwangs, came on together in a group, starting with an elderly couple who had to hold on to each other every now and then to keep from falling. After them came a big woman who swayed heavily onto her right foot when she walked. Rosa noticed now how every time she did the soft parts of her body would rock over to that side like water sloshing in a bathtub. A dark man, her husband, came next to her, tall and strong like an oak tree. He had to be strong, because half the time his wife had to lean her weight on him.

A younger woman came next, kind of like a miniature version of Mrs. Kwang—maybe a sister, only not as big. From the front you could see she had one eye missing, with a black hole instead. If you saw her from the side with her good eye, she still looked kind of pretty. She was leading three little kids in a line down the aisle, holding the oldest's hand. The kids followed after her in a train, the very littlest trailing along at the end holding the paw of a stuffed *Torture-Me* Doll. Now Rosa could see that its ear and part of its face had been chewed off, and the smell of its skin made her feel a little sick. All of them sat together over two rows. They made a lot of noise.

Next came a woman with a tennis-racket case. She was about the same age as Rosa's Mamma, with a bandana wrapped around her head. The tennis-racket case was the only thing she carried. She put it on the rack above her head and sat down, but she kept looking up at it every few minutes, like she wanted to make sure it stayed put. When she noticed Rosa looking at her she smiled. Rosa wouldn't smile back.

The last three people to get on the bus were a Chinese couple traveling with a young woman who must have been their daughter. Everyone was shocked at how pretty she was. Even Firoz sat up when these folks came in. You usually never saw anyone that good-looking who wasn't part of the Corporation. By her face, she could have been a commercial-girl.

Those three kept near the front of the bus, and when they sat down there wasn't any more room. The whole bus was full of luggage and tires and spare parts and some food rations that were beginning to spoil. There was a little path to the bathroom, but when Rosa went back there she saw that it was just a seat over a potty hole that went straight to the street. You could probably feel a breeze when you went, and it would be even worse when the bus was moving.

When the driver got on she turned to slip into her chair. She didn't speak to them at all, didn't check their vouchers, didn't look to see if everyone was there. She just pulled the door closed and started up the long, slow ramp that took them from 285 to 85 going north. It went way high, higher than Rosa had ever been in the sky before, and for a minute, looking back out the window, she could see all the way to the City Proper, the whole skyline, just like when you flew over it in commercials.

The 285 looked like a cast-off crust of bread with ants crawling around on it. Rosa could see it wind away into the distance to the east, full of stalls with swarms of people living on the old expressway. Just past the curve was Stone Mountain, with all the solar panels reflecting the afternoon sun, winking and blinding her. Scattered south across the skyline beyond the forest were tiny golden prayer arches growing smaller and smaller as they spread out towards the horizon. Then the bus came down and the view was cut off.

They drove for a while pretty quiet. The bus hummed and shook like an overfull washing machine, but it seemed it was going to hold together all right. Nobody used this road anymore except veeps and Uniforms, so there weren't any other vehicles in sight, just them cruising up the middle of ten lanes all by themselves. You could see the train tracks off to the side with trains rushing past them to the north.

Everybody was talking just to the people they knew, everybody except for Firoz, who didn't talk to anybody, and the lady with the tennis-racket case who looked like she was listening to something. Rosa didn't know what it could be; she couldn't hear anything except the bus. Whatever the woman heard, she seemed to be enjoying it a lot. She just grinned and tapped her fingers on the seat next to her.

They drove like that for about half an hour. Rosa looked out the window at the vast stretches of outer Atlanta. It looked pretty much like what she knew. Neighborhood after neighborhood after neighborhood, people walking, people sitting on curbs, strip malls turned into houses, houses turned into supermarkets. Some parts looked nice; other places looked pretty bad. There were blocks dressed up to look proud, surrounded on all sides by old and dead buildings.

The bus driver pulled out onto a ramp leading to a collection of cottages that had snuck up on them. She pulled off to the side of the road. Then she stood up and turned around. She was kind of short. She had straight black hair pulled back into a bun. It just barely peeked out under her blue cap. Her face was pock-marked and tan, and it was perfectly round. She was pretty old, but she looked solid, firm, like if you ran into her she wasn't going to be the one to fall. "We're coming into Georgiatown," she said. She spoke with a little accent Rosa didn't recognize. "Anybody wants to buy anything, exchange anything, or talk to anyone, you have to do it now. We can't stop anywhere on the route. Also" —she looked them all in the eye, one by one — "anyone who wants to get off, now's the time, okay?" She was quiet for a second, just looking at them. Then she said, "I'm not going to lie to you. It's a very dangerous trip. You know that. You want to get off, do it here. I wouldn't recommend changing your mind in the Unincorporated States." She stopped again. She looked down at the floor of the bus. Then she looked up and said, "We don't give refunds." She turned around, eased back into her seat, and pulled the bus back on the ramp towards Georgiatown.

Buildings appeared outside the bus windows. Georgiatown had started as a mall. Then during the Correction people started living there, building on top of it. Finally it got so crowded it became its own little Proper. Now it looked like a wedding cake: a group of tall, skinny buildings rising out of one huge base. It was exclusive, like the Proper, but people like Rosa could still visit if they had enough number.

The bus pulled up to a curb and everyone got out. The old mall was like a ruined, deserted castle here. Rosa had thought they would finally see some Shareholders and walk around with them, that they would get to pretend they were big, powerful people with lots of number, even if it was just for a second. But then Mamma told her that the Corporation people all shopped in a different part of Georgiatown, and they didn't want to mix with people like Rosa's family.

Where they got to go was pretty lousy. A lot of lawyers' kiosks and cheap clothing stalls. But when Rosa looked past the dirt she could tell that it had once been a really pretty place. There had been a big glass window in front of every shop, and some still had beautiful pictures and designs on the door. Some even had the old signs hanging above so you could tell what they used to sell. Rosa spent ten minutes just staring at one that used to be a bridal shop. The sign for it was in English. All around it was a picture of a tall, white woman in a pretty gown that draped all over her feet. Rosa asked her Mamma why they used a white woman in the picture. Mamma said that was a picture of the woman who owned the store. Mamma seemed really nervous now, and she didn't want to answer most of Rosa's questions. She just kept looking around like she wanted to buy something but couldn't decide what to get.

Rosa didn't think they were going to buy anything, but Mamma and Daddy used most of their number for bottles of water. Mamma said their number wasn't any good on the road. So they bought water bottles, because they could be traded in an emergency.

They didn't end up with a lot of bottles.

She didn't have to go on the trip. She could have stayed behind with Basil. But then she would have had to marry him.

He had asked her yesterday. She didn't always hang out with him anymore, because they were both getting older and they lived in very different worlds. She probably wouldn't even have gone with him to see his drug church if she hadn't just gotten into a fight with some of her flesh friends in the cul-de-sac. They had thought it was funny to remind Rosa that her father was a rain collector and she had to pretend she didn't care by walking away. That meant she had to come home before her Mamma had gone to bed.

"Where you been?" Mamma screamed when she saw her coming down the street. Rosa didn't say anything. "I have the *whole neighborhood* looking for you!"

Rosa rolled her eyes. That was the wrong thing to do. Mamma grabbed her. "Ow, bitch!" Rosa said, and that got Rosa slapped. She struggled. "What *wrong* with you?"

"What's wrong with *me?*" Mamma gripped her daughter's arm and shook it back and forth. She was doing like she always did when she was mad. She was about to tell Rosa she couldn't hang out with her friends in the cul-de-sac anymore. Rosa didn't want to have to tell her she wouldn't be hanging out with them anyway, so she pushed off. She ran past her mother and fled into the house. They were in the middle of another blackout, so the lights were all out. In the dark, she found a box of Noke-O's with some little bits still in it and stole them off to her room. She didn't want to see her mother. But it's hard to lock a curtain, and when her Daddy came home, both her parents just walked in.

The power was still out, so Rosa couldn't pretend she was studying on her AVE. "You could *knock*," she said to them.

"Rosa," Daddy said.

She waited for a minute, but he didn't say anything else. She looked over, ready to shout out "What?" and saw her Mamma with tears in her eyes.

"Mamma! *Naz!*" she cursed. "*Okay.* I snuck out. I'm really *sorry*. I'll never do it again." But neither of them said anything, and Rosa wondered just how much trouble she was in.

"Rosa," Daddy finally said again. "Something happened. Something bad."

She blinked. She didn't really understand what "bad" meant.

Mamma crossed herself. "Our President will take care of us," she said quietly.

"Rosa," Daddy whispered.

"What, Daddy?"

"Mamma's—"

"I got laid off," Mamma blurted out, covering up her Daddy's words. She peered at Rosa for a moment. "You know what that means?"

Rosa sat quietly and wouldn't answer.

Her father went on. "I want you to gather up everything that is important to you in the biggest bag you can still carry. We're going to try to get passage on a bus heading to DC tomorrow morning."

"*Tomorrow! DC?*" she yelled. "That a million miles away! We ain' never gonna make it! What about my friends?"

"Last year my cousins who survived the fever made it to DC," Rosa's mother said in a strained voice. "If we can get up there with them, they may be able to help us...find another job."

"But ain' there crazy whites between Atlanta and DC? What about them?"

Rosa's Daddy looked at the floor. Then he looked up at her and said, "Get packed and get some sleep. Don't forget to make sure the lights don't come on when the blackout ends."

For a while Rosa lay in her bed and listened to her parents whisper, whisper. They were fighting again.

At one point her father's voice got loud. "We don't have enough *number* for vouchers!"

"Shhh! I sold some sleep..." said Rosa's Mama, and her voice went really quiet.

"We'll have to forfeit the rest of this week's water to make..." her father went on, his own voice cutting out. After that, Rosa couldn't make out any more, but she knew that things were bad, especially if they were going to lose their water.

When the blackout finally ended, and Rosa's parents were snoring, she was on her AVE cashing commercials. Old fashioned music came on with its heavy drums and ancient samples. Her avatar came up, a little three-dimensional animated girl named Leethe. *"Hi Rosa!"*

She didn't answer. The little girl was just a construct of the Net, there to help her navigate and go to school. It didn't care if she was polite.

"Show me the Young Guns!" she whispered.

"Yo! Yo! Join the Young Guns!" The commercial came up.

She always liked the way it started, the old-fashioned beats, the camera flying over the City Proper. You could see the tall buildings sparkling in the sunlight, surrounded by the canal and all those little blocks of white nothing, and then you were past it and all you could see were the empty lots on the other side that kept people like her out. Rosa loved the way the Proper looked.

The announcer spoke in an official and authoritative voice. *"Join the Young Guns! Defend CUSA against the Axis of Evil. Ya daddy did it, ya granddaddy did it, now it your turn, bra!"*

Then she got to see the Young Guns in action, running all around her, firing sprayers at enemy combatants, smiling, looking slick. There was this one soldier with hazel eyes she saw every time in that commercial. You could see him up close, good teeth. When Rosa was a little girl she used to fantasize about being married to him. There were female soldiers in the commercial, too. They looked tough, slick, confident.

"*We all in this together.*" Fade to black.

"*Are you thirsty? Look at this, Rosa!*" Now the AVE showed a bunch of stuff on a golden shelf that Rosa would never get to own: better shoes, better clothes, better AVE. Rosa pulled out of the sensation-envelope and lay back on her bed, only able to hear the AVE now.

"What am I going to do, Leethe?" she asked her avatar.

"*What's wrong, Rosa?*"

"I got to leave. I got to leave Atlanta."

She didn't want to leave Atlanta. Maybe she could run off tonight and join the Young Guns. Would they take her? She imagined herself in that uniform, coming home, telling her Mamma and Daddy that it was going to be all right, that she'd take care of them now.

"Where are you going?"

"DC."

"Don't worry, Rosa. We can hook up again when you get there! Look! I tallied all your friends! They're going to miss you while you're offline!"

Rosa heard a what sounded like a rock bouncing off her window. She looked over but didn't see anything through the bars except a roach. She peeked behind the curtain to see if her parents were asleep.

They were currently living in the dining room of a McMansion in the Mt. Paran neighborhood. That room, their living space, was divided in two by a big piece of splintered plywood which separated the front half of the dining room which they used as a kitchen from the back half where they slept. There was also a little curtain between her parents' bedroom and hers.

After her little brother died from toxic fever, she had gotten the room to herself. Rosa's room was farthest from the kitchen so she couldn't sneak out the front door without her parents hearing. But she had a window which opened up on a weedy backyard lawn. The yard was a risky place to go because Mamma could see the lawn too. But there was a big broken fountain with a huge crack in it, and as long as she could get to that fountain without Mamma seeing, she could hide behind it until she knew no one was looking. Then she could slip down the hillside and go around the side of the house next door.

The window was supposed to be locked, but Rosa had broken the latch a year ago and nobody ever bothered to fix it. There were bars on the outside, but they were loose. Rosa had sprayed some lubricant on them one time, and now they swung, without squeaking, far enough for her to get out.

Everything went pretty smoothly this time. She got out the window and made it to the fountain. She ducked down under the disinfected clothes hanging on the line and slid down a bank of grass into the woods behind her house. She didn't want any of the other parents to see her either because she knew they'd tell her Mamma. She had to be careful 'til she got all the way around the condemned house next door. After that, it was a straight shot out to the street.

Basil was there. She could see the red tip of his cigarette, and he held it out to her as she came close.

"Whatchu doin?" he asked her.

"*Nada*," she said as she took the cigarette. She kept quiet for a minute. She noticed he looked uncomfortable, like his muscles were sore. "You get hurt?" she asked him. He was a thirteen-year old apprentice to his father, a Church Padre. Sometimes the Padre was strict with him.

"Nah," he said. "I get in trouble all the time."

She didn't say anything for a long time. "We leavin'," she finally told him. Then she felt like crying.

"Leavin'." He seemed surprised. He looked down at his feet and watched her through the side of his eyes. "Why?"

"Mamma lose her job."

He whistled. "What you goh' do?"

"We don't know," she said.

"You ain't got no place to go?" he repeated.

"Gaw, you quick," she said.

"Don't be cold," he said back. Rosa just stared. Then she held his cigarette out to him.

"Where you goh' go?" he finally asked, taking the butt back.

"DC," she said.

"DC," he repeated, like he couldn't believe it. "Why you go there?"

"We got cousins."

Basil didn't say anything, but he was being quiet in a different way. He looked pretty agitated. "You come to Church?" he finally said.

"To Church?" Rosa said after him. It was hard not to laugh. "My father, he never go there."

"We take people in," he said. "It part of our mission."

"My Daddy even knew you was here, he prob'ly throw me out."

"You be better off," Basil said.

"What *that* supposed to mean?"

Basil shrugged. He seemed to be struggling with something. "I know some shit," he finally said.

"What?" Rosa demanded.

Basil looked like he didn't want to answer. "All I know is that it ain't safe not to have a job."

"Whatchu mean?"

Basil looked up at Rosa. "You come live with me," he said. "Forget your parents. You come marry me."

"What? *Marry* you?"

Basil tried not to look embarrassed at the way she responded. He turned a little angry. "You can laugh if you want," he said. "But it ain't safe not to have no job. You stay with your parents, you see. One day someone come—"

Something began pounding in Rosa's ears. She couldn't listen. "Our President take care of us!" she screamed, to block out his voice. She had forgotten it was the middle of the night and she was outside. "*Vaya,* punk! I never want to see you ugly ass again."

She turned and ran. He chased her, grabbed her wrist, and pulled. "Wait, Rosa, wait!"

She allowed herself to be pulled, even yanked around. She looked at him hard, her wrist in his hand. "What?"

He held out a little gold chain to her.

"What that?"

"A chain. Like a promise. You think about it?"

Without answering or returning his gaze, Rosa took the chain. After a quick look, she stuffed it in her pocket.

They both stood there quiet, like there was more to say. Finally, Basil said it, but it wasn't what Rosa expected.

"You want to come see the Church?"

When she heard him say that, her breath rushed out of her like the air out of an opened balloon. "Your Church?"

"Yes."

"I thought you wasn't allowed to show me that."

That was because she was *chuseno* and her father would shit bricks if he even knew she was talking about it.

"Padre ain't gon' like it."

"Then why..."

"Because if you thinking of going out there where the crazy white people live, you better have another choice."

So she took her neighbor's bike which was always lying there on the floor by their door and she followed Basil around the kids playing tennis in the streets, down twisty Mount Paran towards Long Island in the middle of the night, trying to ignore the distant gunshots a couple of miles away on Roswell Road.

Basil's Church was a little grey stone building on Glen Crest, about a 30-minute ride from her apartment.

The Church wasn't very big. There couldn't have been more than two rooms inside, or maybe three. There were some ruins behind it, some old shell of a building that used to be part of the Church but now wasn't anything but a place for grass to grow. The Church building was old, probably been there since before Rosa's grandmama was a kid.

In front of it was a cemetery with faded gravestones. Rosa ran her hand across one as they passed. In the dark, she could barely make out a "1902" on one.

"Get down!" Basil said, and he threw his bike to the side and pulled Rosa behind a gravestone. They fell onto the grass, and Basil looked around the stone like someone would shoot them if they peeked their heads out.

"Whatchu do that for?" Rosa demanded, dusting herself off.

"Quiet, *perra!*" he whispered at her.

"Don't call me *perra!*" she snapped at him. She smiled inside. To Rosa, it felt just like they were going out. He was just trying to impress her by being a *macho.*

He leaned his back against the gravestone. Then he looked at her. "You pretty," he said. He grinned uncertainly. He brought his hand up to touch her arm.

"Go 'way, Basil," she said, pushing off his arm.

"Why you be like that?" he asked her.

She stopped fighting and let him touch her a little. It felt nice. His face got soft, kinda curious. Rosa knew what he was curious about. Before he could think too much about that, she said, "You goh' take me in or not?"

He looked like he wasn't sure anymore, but he wasn't going to back down. "You sure you want to?" he asked her again.

Rosa nodded. But she was scared, too.

"Stay close to me," he whispered, and he turned onto his belly and crept around the gravestone.

Rosa followed him through the scrub grass and white stone pillows until they were right up behind the old grey building.

She could see stained glass windows along the side of the Church. A little light was coming through them so that they glowed dully. She wondered if they looked prettier from the inside.

Meanwhile, Basil was checking something out by a thickly painted white door near the back. Suddenly a loud bell from somewhere high above them rang out. The sound made Basil panic, and he jumped, looking all around. "Let's go!" he whispered, and vanished through the doorway.

From over the hill, Rosa saw some shapes emerge out of the dark into the glow of the street lamps. They all moved towards the Church, coming from every direction. Each one had a different kind of walk. One kept his head way up and had a conversation with the sky. Others skated with their feet and never took their eyes off the ground. Then there were some who could have been normal if you didn't know.

All these people were the faithful come to worship.

Basil grabbed her hard by the arm and yanked her inside.

She didn't have a chance to complain about being treated rough. She was too scared to make any noise at all. They were *in the Church*. Rosa wasn't supposed to be here. She wasn't even supposed to be within sight of here.

They crept up an old flight of wooden stairs. She knew Basil was sweating it every time a step creaked. Finally they got to the top and, creeping on their hands and knees, they went out onto some kind of balcony with a high wooden rail. She couldn't have seen over without standing up, but she could hear all sorts of shuffling and muttering from down below, only the words didn't make any sense. It sounded like seventy people having seventy different conversations. But it was quiet, too, like nobody answered anybody else, like everyone in that place thought they were the only one there.

They kept creeping 'til they got to the middle of a big dent in the floor that was a different color from the other wood, like something big had once been sitting in that spot. Rosa saw some old wires splayed around, the sliced pieces of rubber-insulation sticking up like two crazy hands. Basil curved his finger at her and pointed her to a little hole in the dent just big enough for the two of them to peek through. They had to keep their faces real close to one another to see. Ordinarily she'd like that, being close to him, but this time she was too scared.

Down below she could see a very long room stretching out with rows and rows of benches all facing some raised platform. There were a couple of high tables, and on each table many bags and bottles. In front stood two people dressed in black robes with hoods behind their heads, waiting patiently while two lines formed, made up of all the addicts who had been walking towards the Church.

"What they doing?" Rosa whispered to Basil.

"That the faithful lining up to get the Body and the Blood," Basil answered.

"What that?"

"What they need. Whatever drugs they on."

"How you know what drugs they need?"

"It our *job* to know," Basil said, trying to sound wise.

Now each person in line was stepping up and showing them their arm or opening their mouth, and the robe-people were applying tourniquets or giving them whatever it was they asked for.

"We got to learn about seventy different kinds of drugs," Basil told her, "and they got to be the *right* ones or the faithful can die or lose control."

Rosa didn't know what to say. She just watched it for a while. It made her feel taller inside, seeing something that she knew her Mamma and Daddy never saw.

Basil squawked, and out of the corner of her eye Rosa saw him being pulled away. She was too terrified to look up until she heard the other deep, dry voice.

"This is abomination," it said. Right after came a hand hitting somebody's face. That's when Rosa turned around real quick and scooted away, looking up at the Padre, Basil's father.

He looked down at her. "You don't belong here!" he admonished. "Why are you in the building?"

Rosa didn't know how to answer. Did he know she was *chuseno?* What would he say if he found out?

She saw Basil with his face all twisted up, and she could tell by that look that he was going to get it and he didn't want her to see. So before he could ask her another question she ran out the room, down the stairs and out and away from the building.

The bike ride back was much harder and scarier. The only light came from the few telephone pole AVEs that hadn't burned out or been smashed with a rock. When she got back to her house, wheezing and sweating, she slipped back up the hill, pulled the bars open and slipped in. Without a word to her Avatar, she slid under her blanket.

She lay there in the darkness, thinking. Should she get her things and go back? Back to Basil and a new life at the Church?

Pendejo. Marry her! He just wanted to see her naked. Rosa couldn't believe she'd ever liked him.

And by 5 AM the next day she and her parents were on the I-285 with a crowd of people, walking their way around the arc to trade what they had for little paper vouchers to get on the bus. And now Rosa was wondering if she should have taken him up on it.

The bus driver said her name was Chassis. She didn't say much after that. Rosa wanted to go over to ask her questions, but she stayed near Daddy instead, who had taken a seat opposite her and Mamma in the same row. He was looking at Firoz like he hadn't seen him before.

"What's the matter, Daddy?"

"Nothing," he said. He just glared. Meanwhile, Firoz wasn't looking back. He was still gazing out the window, looking exactly like he did when he first sat down.

Rosa was nervous about the way Mamma and Daddy were acting, and she wanted to get away from them for a while. She tried to get up and move to the front of the bus, but Mamma put her heavy arm around her and kept her close. After about twenty minutes, the bus slowed down. Rosa thought Chassis was going to pull over, but she just stopped under a covered booth. She leaned out the window and started chatting with a woman in the gate. Real friendly. Chassis had her head out the window for maybe fifteen minutes. Rosa never heard a word, but she heard Chassis laughing. Chassis' laugh sounded like two bricks scraping together, a quality that could put you on edge or make you feel real safe, depending on whose side you were on.

The woman in the booth came out and walked around the back of the bus. She walked slow, Rosa guessed, because she was checking things. Rosa wondered if she was going to look up the potty hole.

Finally, she got to the door and Chassis let her on. She was wearing a black and gold body suit with gold stripes down the side. She was heavy like Chassis, but a whole lot younger. Her wiry hair was cropped short under a tight cap with a brim that shaded her eyes. Mamma and Daddy got nervous again, but this woman didn't look like she would cause them any trouble. She didn't look like she even saw any of them. She just started talking in this dead voice.

"You are about to leave the Corporation of the United States of America. This bus is headed for the MidAtlantic Protectorate. You are expected to remain on this bus until it reaches its route."

She sounded like she'd said this stuff five million times already, maybe even five million times today. She sounded like she didn't care if they lived or died.

"CUSA makes no claim of your safety. Anyone traveling over the Unincorporated States by land does so at their own risk. Once you cross the border behind me, your electronic signatures will be deactivated for security purposes. Your connection to CUSA exists entirely in your voucher. For this reason, if your voucher is lost or damaged, you will not be allowed back into CUSA.

"This is for your own safety."

She looked around at them like she was waiting for somebody to argue. Nobody said anything.

"As citizens and protectees of CUSA, you will be allowed back into CUSA territory upon presentation and surrender of your voucher. You must surrender your voucher to re-enter CUSA."

She stopped again. It was like the pauses were part of the speech or something.

"CUSA is not liable for anything lost or damaged in the Unincorporated States. Any disputes arising in or with the Unincorporated States must be taken up with the Office of Foreign Affairs in Baltimore. This includes all loss of property and/or life. Are there any questions?"

"When do we eat?" asked the woman with the tennis-racket case. Everybody on the bus chuckled. Even Chassis.

The border lady nodded like she thought the joke was okay, but she didn't smile. "Have a good day," she said. Then she stepped off.

Chassis pulled the bus through the booth, and they started heading for an underpass. They went underneath a big road that Rosa could see had a bunch of fences and barbed wire on it. "That's the outer loop," said Daddy. "Are you ready?" He looked over at her and ran his fingers through Rosa's hair. That irritated Rosa, and she shook him off.

They went through three gates that were tucked under the tunnel. Once they got through, Rosa tried to look back, but she couldn't see behind them because the bus didn't have a rear window and Mamma wouldn't let her open theirs.

On the outer side of the loop everything was really green. Rosa was surprised. Nobody lived out here. Nobody. No Churches, no buildings, no houses. Just the road and a bunch of trees and weeds. At first, when they went under bridges, you could sometimes see old towers or something, but after a while it just looked dark and green.

They rode for a while with everybody keeping their seats. Rain started tapping on the windows. The tap became a torrent, the rain pounding against the roof of the bus, the hard wind occasionally rocking the bus. Rosa sat with her cheek in the crook of Mamma's arm and watched the scenery through the white curtains of water. She thought about lots of things, about nothing. She wished she had an AVE to log on to. She wanted a cigarette bad enough that she didn't care if Mamma and Daddy finally found out she had started smoking.

The Kwang children had started getting up, making even more noise. Mamma Kwang and Aunt One-Eye tried to keep them in their seats, but Mr. Kwang didn't do much or say much. He just sat there like his oak-tree self and kept quiet, letting his women do all the work. After a while Mamma and One-Eye got tired of slapping the older one on top of the head, tired of yanking around the littlest by the arm, and they fell back in their seats and let them run.

Nobody seemed to mind. The kids were noisy, but they weren't bad, mostly just coming up to different people and staring at them.

The Chinese family were too polite to look unhappy when the kids came up. The really pretty young girl played with the middle child and made him giggle. Then when he started squealing she tried to send him away, but he wouldn't leave.

The tennis-racket-case lady was always smiling. Rosa wanted to know what she was so happy about. She acted like she was proud, like the kids were hers, the way she caught the eye of grandpa Kwang. He smiled too and nodded quickly, showing his yellow, broken teeth, but he didn't look her in the eye.

The oldest kid and the youngest came to the back of the bus. First they went down to Firoz and checked him out. He didn't seem to notice them. He hadn't moved since he sat down. He was still staring out the window like those trees outside were really something interesting. The kids tried to get his attention by playing near him, then by poking him with their fingers and running away fast. He didn't move, not even to scratch.

Finally, they got bored and came up to Rosa. Mamma and Daddy smiled at them, but they were looking at her.

"I'm Samoae," said the littlest one.

Rosa nodded.

"Where you from?" the oldest one asked.

"Buckhead," Rosa said. The tattered doll the littlest one was carrying smelled horrible up close. It reeked a combination of sock sweat and chikin soup. Samoae held it up for Rosa to see. *"I'll tell! I'll tell!"* it said, to keep the child from torturing it.

"Where you from?" Rosa asked him.

"Fairburn," he said.

Rosa knew about Fairburn. It was rough down there. Lots of old strip-malls falling apart, with people living in them.

"Come play!" Samoae asked her. Rosa didn't want to be near the doll, but Mamma patted her to go, so she went. They took her up to introduce her to the Grandma and Grandpa, then the Mamma and Daddy, then the one-eyed lady they called Aunt Kin.

The pretty Chinese girl at the front of the bus was still trying to get the middle child to go away, but he wouldn't go. The other two finally pulled Rosa up to where he was, and she and Samoae and the older one all bounced on the seats, laughing and making lots of noise.

Rosa and her friends settled on the row in front of the Chinese girl's parents and stared at them for a while. Rosa never would have been allowed to stare if she hadn't been sitting with the Kwang kids, who were too young to know better. Rosa got a good look at them.

They didn't look like much now, but she was getting the idea they used to be pretty number, just from the way they sat. They looked uncomfortable, but they tried to pretend they weren't, as if the spongy seats were some kind of couch they were reclining on and this was a royal bus. Most Chinese, maybe all of them, lived in the City Proper, usually high up. Rosa didn't know what could have happened to these people to make them leave their home. Their clothes were old and faded, but they would have been expensive if they'd been new.

The man kept his eyes far away. The woman would look back and smile really sweet, then look down. She did this three times. Rosa knew the Chinese people were uncomfortable, but she just couldn't resist getting a good stare at someone, especially someone interesting. Finally, the Chinese woman tried to make friends.

"What are your names?"

The Kwang kids wouldn't answer. Rosa waited for a second, and then she said, "Rosa."

"What does your father do, Rosa?" she asked.

Rosa didn't want to tell her that her Daddy had been out of work so long. "He works for the neighborhood," she said.

"What does your mother do?"

"She was a code checker," Rosa said. "But she lost her job and now we're going up to DC to find a new one."

The woman nodded. "That's what happened to me, too," she said.

"Really?" Rosa asked.

"I worked for Noke," she said. "In antivirals."

Little Samoae had started stroking the hair of the Chinese daughter. "It so black an' smooth! Like night!" The daughter tried to sit there like she didn't mind it, and the parents were making like it didn't bother them either because nobody wanted to hurt Samoae's feelings.

Rosa wanted to break the ice, distract them. "Noke? Wow! Us too! That's who Mamma worked for. Did you live in the City Proper?"

"We did," she said.

"That must have been great," Rosa said. "We just lived in Buckhead. Do you have a brand?" Rosa knew her mother would go crazy if she found out she'd asked someone about their tattoo, but her mother wasn't here, and she really wanted to see one.

The woman nodded again.

"Can I see it?" Rosa begged. The Kwangs stood up on the seats, interested. "Can we see it?" echoed Samoae, jumping up and down so hard her voice started to jiggle.

The woman reached up to her shoulder and pulled a flap away. Underneath was a pattern of blue bars. It looked like an air-conditioner vent. Members of the Corporation all had one implanted under their skin, and it had all sorts of stuff about them on it, even how much number they had.

She elbowed her husband. "Show them yours," she told him.

He did what she told him. His tattoo looked a lot like hers. You could see the hair growing all over it. "Don't you have to shave that for it to work, mister?" asked the oldest Kwang.

The man glowered and looked away. The woman answered for him. "We don't use them anymore." The man turned on her suddenly like he wanted to argue, but she shut him up just by looking at him.

Rosa wanted to ask more, but she got a feeling that her Mamma would really pull her away now. The Kwang kids had already gone down the aisle, and Rosa wanted to follow them. "See you," she said to the Chinese woman.

By the time Rosa got to the middle of the bus, the three Kwang kids were all gathered around and the tennis-racket-case lady was showing them something.

Rosa crept over and peeked across the seat. She couldn't believe what the woman had taken out of the case: It was made of orange wood, shaped like a kidney bean, with a scrape down near where her hand touched the strings. Rosa couldn't look away. She'd never seen a tennis racket like that before.

"What is that?" asked the middle child, who had never seen one.

"It's called a guitar. People used to play them. Want to hear a commercial?"

"Can I play?" the oldest asked.

"Rosa!" her Mamma called.

"I have to go," Rosa told them. The woman started *"I'd like to teach the world to sing..."* while Rosa went back to her Mamma and Daddy. She noticed that Firoz had fallen asleep against the window. The rain seemed to pour into his head as it fell in sheets along the glass.

"I'd like to buy the world a Coke..." continued the voice of the guitar woman.

"What are you doing?" Mamma asked her.

"Nothing," Rosa said. She sat down next to her Mamma and leaned on her arm. Mamma pulled the arm out and wrapped it around her so she was fully surrounded by it.

The darkness had come in on the rain.

Rosa didn't think she was tired, but when she woke up she couldn't see at first, feeling the bus bouncing under her. She didn't know how long she had been asleep, but everyone was quiet now. When her eyes adjusted, she noticed that even the little kids in front had gone down. Only the bus driver was awake, looking all around as she drove, even though she was just looking into the blackness.

Mamma was still asleep. Rosa carefully slid out from under Mamma's arm and started walking towards the front of the bus. The bus driver's comfy chair was set just a little below the floor, and she moved all around in it as she drove, like she was dancing on her bottom. When the driver heard Rosa coming she looked up out of her little cockpit. Rosa wasn't sure if she was allowed to come up, but the driver didn't say anything. She just turned back around and kept dancing.

There were a lot of interesting things in Chassis' cockpit. All in front of her were dials and switches, some that were lit up, others dark. Some of the big switches were obviously missing, and some metal pieces were showing where plastic used to be on top. Along her left side were a bunch of old photographs taped to the wall. Rosa couldn't make out the images in them because they were really small and they didn't move. She wanted to get closer to see them, but she thought it would be rude.

Finally Rosa noticed the little box by Chassis' left hand that buzzed like it had bees inside. Then instead of buzzing, it squawked.

"What's that?" Rosa pointed at it.

Chassis looked at Rosa's finger. "The radio," she said. "Old-time AVE."

"Oh," Rosa said.

"You've been asleep five hours," Chassis said. "You should go back to sleep."

"When are we going to be there?" Rosa asked.

"By noon tomorrow. Maybe sooner. It depends."

"On what?" Rosa asked.

"Lots of things," she said. "I know the roads really well, but things change out here. Depends on the route."

Rosa nodded like she understood. She tried to look smart because she had decided she liked Chassis and wanted to impress her.

"You log on to school?" the driver asked her.

"Yeah," Rosa said.

"What Game?"

"They up to *Ultimate Acquisition VII.*"

"They still play *UA?* You like it?"

"It's okay." Rosa said, shrugging. "I wouldn'a chose it, but that's the one they assigned for my neighborhood." Before the driver could ask her another question, Rosa said, "Where you from?"

"I'm from everywhere," Chassis said.

"No you ain't," Rosa said, waving her head around.

"Yeh I is," she said in Spank.

That surprised her. Rosa answered her in Spank. "How you learn to talk like that?"

"Spank been 'round a lot longer than you!"

"You don't look like you speak Spank!"

"That 'cause Mamma 'Bangladeshi!" she said. "But I been 'roun'."

"You Bangladeshi?" Rosa asked.

"Mmm hmm."

"From there?"

"When I was little."

"How little?"

"Littler than you!" and she smiled. "We gone right before Bangladesh get taken."

"You remember?"

"Nothin' to remember," she said, shaking her head. "I been lots of other places since then."

"Where you go?"

"Everywhere!"

"Where?"

"You name it."

"Washington."

"Uh huh." she said.

"Ex-Houston."

"Mmm hmm."

"LA."

"Yep."

"How you go so many places?" Rosa asked her.

"'Cause I done so many things."

"Like what?"

She didn't answer. She was slowing down. She was looking at something in her headlights. She cussed in some language Rosa didn't know.

"There's a bridge out," she said in Spanish. "It's collapsed."

"How you get round it?" Rosa asked her.

"Wait," she said. She reached down and grabbed a little box off of the squawking thing. It was attached with a funny piece of coiled rubber. She talked into it, quiet, so Rosa couldn't really hear.

The box squawked back at her, and Rosa caught a little of it. Whoever was squawking told Chassis they didn't know about the collapse.

"It must be a recent one," she said. "They go out all the time, now. They're finally beginning to fall apart."

"How you get round it?" Rosa asked her again.

"We go up this ramp and down the other one," said Chassis. She was looking around more intently now, like she was trying to see through the dark. She moved the big wheel at her chest to the right, and the bus pulled over and started turning around. She took them back up the way they'd come and then wheeled the bus onto the ramp.

"What you used to do?" Rosa asked to get back to the conversation.

"Everything."

"Like what?"

"When I was just a little older than you, I got my first job. I used to monitor websites for illegal activity. You know what websites are?"

Rosa nodded her head, even though she didn't.

"Then I made deliveries in the boondocks."

"The what?"

"I delivered things for people like those that live in the shacks on the I-285."

"Oh," Rosa said. "Like what?"

She smiled. "And I was a swimming instructor. You swim?"

Rosa shook her head.

"No, of course you don't," said Chassis, shaking her head at herself. "I forget sometimes about pools." She went on. "I drove my first bus when I was twenty-three. Took it all the way to Chicago— " Her voice died. She was looking ahead at the road. There wasn't any ramp back down. Just trees. She cussed again.

"What is it?"

"There's no return access ramp," she said. "Now I have to figure out where...wait a minute." She talked into her radio again and waited. The radio squawked back at her, and she nodded. Then she smiled. "Okay," she said. "I know where we are. That's fine. That will even save us some time."

"What?" Rosa asked, curious.

"I know a good route we can take," she said, and she started moving the bus to the right, down the road into the darkness.

"Is it all like this?" Rosa asked. It looked even darker through the windows than it did along the highway, if that was possible.

"Like what?"

"Woods. Woods."

"No," Chassis said, cocking her head. "There's some cities out here."

"*Cities?*" Rosa said. "In the US?"

"Sure," Chassis said, moving her hands up and down the steering wheel. "Richmond is still pretty big. Charlotte. Wheeling. They even have electricity."

"No way!"

Chassis laughed hard. "What they teach you in that game you play now?"

Rosa shrugged. "We learn about the President, how great he is, how he gonna take care of us..."

"Yeah, yeah," Chassis said, like she'd heard it all before. Rosa raised her eyebrows. She was surprised that Chassis wasn't more respectful. "What else?"

"We learn about what we need to do to get a job, who we need to talk to, how we get around, how we stay safe..."

"Don't you learn any history?"

"Sure," Rosa said. "We learn about the Dow and the Great Correction and how the President saved us."

Chassis chewed her lip. "Huh," she said. "So they don't teach you any history."

"What you mean?" Rosa demanded.

"You know why the whites left?"

Rosa was quiet for a minute. Then she admitted, "No."

Chassis waited like she wanted her to ask. Rosa wanted to know, but she didn't want to sound any dumber than she felt. So she kept quiet. Finally, Chassis said, "You know what the Correction *was?*"

Rosa shrugged. She thought she did.

Then Chassis started rattling off facts like she was an AVE and Rosa was buying. "Back in the old days people didn't have tattoos, and the credit companies weren't part of the government, so you could get into a lot more trouble with your number and nobody would mess with you. One time millions of people made a stupid mistake with their money at the same time and the economy collapsed."

Rosa didn't understand every word Chassis was saying, but she was really interested in the story anyway, since nobody had ever bothered to tell her true facts about history.

Chassis went on. "Things got better for a while, but then they went bad again. Up and down, a bunch of falls, each one worse than the last. They take all of them together and call them the Correction. That would have been bad enough.

"But out west, the Colorado River had dried up because of the heat, and everyone left Las Vegas, pushing into the East Coast and West Coast. Right about then the ocean levels were getting high enough that when a bad bunch of storms hit the East Coast, all the major cities out there got flooded. New York, Baltimore, DC. The levels never did come down again, and everybody was just stuck."

Chassis could have been making up a rhyme. She was looking left and right into the darkness, checking the invisible road, bouncing up and down on her seat. And all the while her story just flowed out of her.

"The people with all the number got out, you know? They fled to higher ground. That was happening anyway, though. After Iran took Mexico in, a lot of Mexican Catholics fled north, into the big dry cities where their families were.

"So when the government became a Corporation and changed USA into CUSA, it was mostly darker people living there.

"Then they built the levies around DC, and the walls around the Southern Protectorate, the Northern Protectorate, the Texas Protectorate...you know them all, right?"

Rosa nodded. Yes, she knew all the Protectorates. She was glad she knew *something*, anyway.

"Well, Richmond and those other cities got left out. Charlotte almost made it, but they had a *coup* and the President didn't want to waste his number protecting it anymore. So now it's one of those Unincorporated States.

"They got electric power," Chassis said, getting back to that subject. "Though you can't rely on it out there like you can in

CUSA. There are lots of blackouts and things, especially when someone tries to take over as Governor, but it's not as bad as out in the country where they make do with candles or garbage."

"Do the Young Guns protect them too?" Rosa asked.

"*The Young Guns?*" Chassis said really loud. "CUSA's not going to use its troops and its number protecting a million little backwards White States, even if they are all gathered in one big place. No, they're just out there, like the little towns in the woods."

Before Chassis could go any further, Rosa heard a noise from the back of the bus. Chassis looked into her mirror. Rosa couldn't believe the noise, because she recognized the voice. It was her father. He was screaming at Firoz.

Rosa couldn't see what Firoz was doing because her father was in the way, hanging over the seat. She quickly ran back there to see what was going on.

"Nobody said you could do that here!" he yelled, his accusing finger pointing down.

Firoz didn't answer him. He just looked out with large eyes. Rosa looked down at his arm and saw the needle hanging from it.

Rosa's father turned towards the front of the bus and began screaming at Chassis. "Nobody told me there was a drug-worshipper on board!"

Now everybody was awake. The little Kwang children and the beautiful young Chinese girl were all looking back at Rosa's father like they couldn't figure out how he had gotten on the bus. Everybody else was trying to ignore him.

"Daddy," Rosa said. "Forget it." She pulled his arm.

"Go sit down, Rosa," Daddy said.

"Daddy—"

"*Sit down!*" He shoved Rosa away so hard that she stumbled and had to catch herself on the hard rubber floor. The lines on the mat cut into her hands. She watched what happened next from the floor.

Rosa's father had turned back to scream some more at the drug addict. "If you don't get that needle out of your arm I'll break your neck, I swear I will! I'll kill you!"

Rosa couldn't see Firoz's response, but before her father could do anything, Chassis stopped the bus so suddenly it jerked everybody forward. Rosa fell over again onto her back.

"What's your problem, mister?" Chassis shouted from the front, rising to her feet.

"Nobody told me there was a drug-worshipper on board!" Rosa's father answered her.

"So what?" the driver said. "He paid his money like you did; he gets to ride on the bus!"

"Not with me!" Rosa's father insisted.

"You want off?" Chassis replied, threateningly.

"I want *him* off!" Rosa's father said, the spit in his throat making his voice rough.

Rosa's Mamma was up by now, and she had pulled Rosa to her feet and out of the aisle. "Eduardo!" she said.

"Nobody gets off this bus unless I throw them out," Chassis said, coming towards Rosa's father.

"No, Kata," he said, holding out his hand, stopping Rosa's mother from coming any closer.

"You need to tell me what your problem is, mister," said the driver. She shoved past Rosa's Mamma and was right in her Daddy's face. He should have been scared, but he was crazy, now, like Rosa saw him only when he was talking about drugs. His black eyes were wide open like big, bottomless pools.

"No prosperity without sobriety," Rosa's father quoted in English. "Genius is 10% inspiration and 90% perspiration!"

"I smell fear!" Firoz answered loudly. It was the first time he had spoken. Rosa could see the addict's face now. He was looking all around like he saw things moving down the walls that frightened him.

"Look, mister, I'll give you one warning," Chassis said. "And then I'm going to throw you out, with or without your wife and daughter." She was tense, like she was getting ready to move on him. Rosa's heart started beating faster. Was Chassis really going to throw her father off the bus?

But Rosa's father didn't seem to have heard the driver. "Your wine is not as my wine!" Rosa's father shouted, pointing at Firoz. "And your bread is not as my bre—"

Something exploded loud enough to drown Rosa's father out. The bus rocked once to the right and stayed there. Rosa tried to keep from falling into the space between the seats.

Chassis braced herself, and then she cursed in Spanish so everyone could tell what she was saying. Rosa didn't like the sound of it, too much panic from the adult she had relied on to keep them together. There was another explosion, and the bus rocked again. Now it was leaning towards the front. By the time Chassis got to the front of the bus, there were four more explosions, and the bus rocked and leaned a different way each time.

Then Rosa heard glass shattering, and Chassis got to the driver's seat front really fast. The pretty Chinese girl started screaming. Rosa noticed that the Kwang kids by contrast didn't make a sound. They had already gotten down behind the seats. Even little Samoae was holding completely still next to her mother. Obviously those kids had been through something like this before.

The bus door shattered into a thousand pieces and folded in. Rosa saw Chassis' eyes were now trained on the large man coming up the stairs with a shotgun in his hands. As he got to the top a little woman stepped up behind him.

The man resembled a huge toddler—his face puffy and pink. His pimply scalp looked like a pig's back. Along the bands of the sleeveless T-shirt he was wearing, you could see lumps of various sizes all over the bottom of his neck and shoulders. He spoke in a voice like the gunshot that had demolished the bus door. "Y'all are trespassing!" He was speaking English, of course. Rosa knew a little English because all the prayers were in English, but his accent was so strange she almost couldn't make it out. "We welcome you to the great sovereign nation of Stake's Claim Under God." He held his gun across his chest.

The old woman creaked out from behind him, "Y'all speak English?" She was tiny compared to the man, but she didn't look fragile. Rosa figured you couldn't get a pin inside the folds of her prim old-fashioned suit. Her steely blue eyes were sweeping from side to side, and knocked away everything they touched. The little grey bun on the back of her head was so tight Rosa thought it must have been glued to her.

"I understand you," said Chassis, stepping up to the man and looking at his face. She didn't seem much afraid. She actually looked like she was trying not to laugh. The man noticed and he glared down at her like he was ready to step on her.

"Any of these other folks?" the old woman asked, nodding with her head at all the passengers.

Chassis shrugged.

"Tell them they've entered our jurisdiction unlawfully, but if they do as they're told, no one will harm them."

Chassis turned back towards them and spoke to them in bored Spanish. "This is obviously a tribute ambush. I'm sorry. It happens from time to time. Just do what I tell you. Don't listen to them. Listen to me."

The old woman waited for a second. "You tell them yet?" she asked Chassis.

"What do you want?" Chassis asked.

"We ask what's fair in the name of the Skelton Treaty," she said. "Ten percent of all valuables on the bus. An' half that good city water you brought, too."

"The Skelton Treaty was repealed," Chassis told her. "Virgilina breached—"

"That's *Virgilina!*" the old woman snapped, showing her sharp teeth, her eyes like cold iron. Rosa couldn't believe how Chassis didn't flinch from her glare. When the woman made her demands she seemed completely unbending, like any answer that wasn't yes was a dangerous one, maybe even too dangerous for her to consider. "We're a sovereign nation unto God, separate from Virgilina. You have a compact with *us*."

Chassis shrugged. Frowning with impatience, the old woman pulled out a little silver pistol and pointed it at Chassis. Looking briefly at the pistol, Chassis turned towards her passengers and said in Spanish, "These people don't want to deal with the work of getting rid of us. They're not necessarily murderers. They just want ten percent of everything you own. That's one tenth of your cigarettes, some of your food, half of your water. Use your common sense and give them something valuable. Don't hold anything back or they'll just get angry. They probably wouldn't mind killing one or two of you."

Quickly the passengers started fishing through their possessions, finding things they could get rid of. When Rosa looked out the window she saw people pointing big guns right at their heads.

"Don't give them just any old thing," Chassis said in Spanish. "It's got to be something that will satisfy them."

"You," the little old woman said to Chassis. "Sit in the chair." She waved the small silver pistol towards the driver's seat.

Chassis nodded and moved past the big man, then eased herself down. "Go on," the woman said in English, and the oversized, greasy baby man started walking down the aisle toward Rosa with an empty burlap sack. He looked over everything people handed him. Sometimes he nodded and took it. Sometimes he shook his head and roared in their faces until they gave him something else. He seemed to be concentrating very hard on his job, his breath loud and steady.

The guitar lady had to open her case and show him what was inside. The man frowned at the guitar like he couldn't tell if it was valuable or not. Then he gestured at the strings. Her face fell and she took the strings off of it, unravelling them one by one like she was undressing a lover. After she gave the strings to the big man she turned away to the window so he couldn't her face.

The man got to Rosa, curled back in her Mamma's grip which grew tighter at his approach. His sweaty, dirty smell got stronger as he leaned forward. He hung over her with an expectant glare. She didn't know what to give him. Instinctively, her hand had already gone into her pocket. Her fingers intertwined with the chain Basil had given her. Quickly she pulled it out and held it up for the man to see. The man grabbed it to look at it real close, then stuffed it in his shirt pocket.

Rosa knew her Mamma had seen the chain and would want to know where she got it. She couldn't ask now, because nobody was talking. Rosa's Mamma gave the man two cigarettes because she didn't want to spare any food. Rosa's father was rummaging through his bag to find anything he could. All he could come up with was a wrapped piece of chocolate.

As the man moved past, Rosa put her knees on the seat and turned to see what he would do when he got to Firoz. The addict probably didn't even know what was going on. "Come on, spig!" the man shouted at him. He slapped Firoz with his huge hand. "Up!" But Firoz didn't look at him. His body just went where the man's hand took it.

"He's a drug worshipper," Chassis told the woman at the front of the bus. "He doesn't have anything but his drugs."

"No food? No *water?*" demanded the woman.

"Probably not," Chassis said.

The big man searched all over Firoz's body, feeling for anything he could take. All he found were needles and empty plastic bags. Roughly he pulled the needle out of Firoz' arm, and he cursed as he tried to avoid the blood oozing from the puncture. He threw the empty syringe to the side and glared down at Firoz.

"He ain't got nothing," the man said back to the woman.

"I told you," Chassis said.

"Then he's got to die," the woman said, shrugging.

"No!" Chassis said, standing up.

"Yes, he *dies!*" the woman shouted at her. "He ain't got no tribute. He's in violation of the treaty. Penalty for going against a treaty agreed upon under God is death!"

"He's in my care," Chassis said to her. "You got plenty. Now you get off."

The woman raised her gun and pointed it at Chassis' head. "You talk to me like that, you ugly old spigger, I'll put a hole in you like—"

"See this?" Chassis gestured towards her radio. "It's on and it's connected to my home base in Atlanta. They've been listening to everything that happened here. They know where we are, because you told them. You harm anyone on this bus, and the Young Guns will come out with sprayers and kill all your sons."

The woman stared thin-eyed at Chassis for a second. She looked at Chassis' feet. Rosa wondered what she was thinking. Was she going to get mad? Could Chassis' threat really stop her when they were all out here in the middle of nowhere?

But the woman nodded. "Okay," she said. "Come on, Porter. Get on up here."

He shambled up to the front of the bus, bumping each seat with his legs and his burlap sack. Just as he got to the front, he noticed the pretty Chinese girl and her parents. He stopped short. The old woman and Chassis both watched as he carefully put his bag on the ground. He reached out, amazed, and ran his hand down the Chinese girl's silky hair. After the second time, she started to tremble. Her mother began talking to her quickly in her own language.

"Look, Mimi," the big man said softly, his voice gentle. "A China doll! Real pretty."

"Come on, Porter," the old woman said, sighing. She suddenly looked very tired, a world of weight behind her eyes.

The Chinese mother was watching the big man stroking her daughter's silk. Rosa never saw anybody so still in her life. She kept her hands from trembling by holding them in little balls in front of her mouth.

"I want this one, Mimi," Porter half asked, looking back at the old lady.

Chassis didn't say anything this time, but the old woman did. "That ain't under the agreement, Porter. Come on."

"I want her," Porter insisted. "For me!"

"No!" the old woman said, patient but firm. "It ain't part of God's agreement with Skelton. We keep our word. One tenth. Now get on!"

"I want her for the night, then!" Porter said. He grabbed a hank of the girl's long hair. The girl screamed. The mother and father cried out and clutched at her.

"No!" the old woman shouted. She moved up the stairs and came right up to Porter. She slapped him hard across the cheek. He let the girl drop to her seat, feeling his face with his hand. "Now we keep our agreements or God takes vengeance," whispered the old lady. "You don't get to take a woman out of marriage."

"But for the night," Porter protested.

"*No!* Not for the night! You follow God's Law!"

Porter stared at his Mimi. Rosa couldn't see his face, and she wondered if he was going to hurt the old lady. But then he sniffled a little bit, turned, and looked around the bus. His eyes fell on Rosa.

The look in them changed from being frustrated to something Rosa didn't want to say. She suddenly remembered what he smelled like, could imagine what it would be like to have his stubble pricking her throat.

"Rosa," muttered her Mamma, like she was thinking the same thing.

All of a sudden, the old lady turned, and her gun went off with a jerk.

The guitar woman lurched as if shocked, then slumped over with a protesting groan. Rosa could see the guitar strings fall to the rubber floor from her hand. She had been trying to take them back out of the burlap sack while the old lady and the big man were arguing. Shot, the guitar woman continued to protest with a helpless shake of her head. Then she was staring at nothing.

The old lady came, picked up the strings from the floor, then put them back in the sack. She looked up at Chassis. "We stick to our agreement," she said. "One tenth." Chassis just nodded and didn't say anything. "Go, Porter," the old lady said to him. "Or I'll shoot a hole in you for the same reason." Porter sagged a little. He moved to the front of the bus and down the stairs.

"You'll have our protection all the way to Ascension," the old lady said to Chassis on the way out. "No one will harm you here. Throw six of your tires out, and my boys will put them on for you."

Chassis nodded again, and she and Rosa's Mamma and Mr. Kwang started throwing tires out the front door. They felt the bus shake some more. Rosa sat and listened to how quiet it was and how loud the pounding of her heart had become. Rosa's Daddy didn't speak. Not about Firoz, not about anything. He just got back in his seat, looked straight ahead and sat really quiet.

Then Chassis started up the bus again and drove them away.

Rosa's father didn't open his mouth after the incident. He didn't say a word to Rosa's Mamma or to Rosa. Mamma was pretending he was okay, but she was tugging obsessively on her own sleeve. Rosa could tell she was pretty shaken up.

"Why isn't Daddy saying anything?" Rosa asked.

"I don't know, sweetie."

"Is it 'cause of Firoz?"

"I don't know, Rosa."

"Why—" She was afraid to ask, because he was sitting right there, but he didn't look like he could even hear what she was saying. "Why do we hate drug people so much?" she whispered into Mamma's ear.

Mamma looked like she didn't think Daddy was listening, either. She shrugged, and she looked really tired. "I wasn't *chuseno* before I married your father," she said. "His grandparents were true believers." Mamma shifted like she was uncomfortable. "Drugs weren't legal when my mother was a child the way they are now."

"But why do we hate them?"

Mamma didn't answer directly. "Your Daddy was raised that way, and it's just in him forever. They put it in him really hard."

"Is he gonna be okay?"

Mamma nodded. "Yes, honey. Drink a sip of your water."

"I don't want to." Rosa didn't ask any more questions. She didn't think Mamma wanted to answer any more anyway.

"Daddy," Rosa said, quietly, patting him on the arm. But he looked like he didn't feel or hear.

The bus was moving through the dark again. After a while, Rosa got up and walked towards Chassis at the front. On the way she saw the other families. They were hunkered down together. The Kwangs were talking with each other too quiet to hear with the wind whistling through the busted door. The old couple were asleep on each other's shoulders. The kids were playing already. If what had just happened didn't faze them, Rosa hated to think what they had been through.

Rosa didn't look at the body of the guitar lady as she passed. Even out of the corner of her eye she could still see the blood pooling on the floor under the seat. The smell of the fresh blood made her stomach churn. Rosa rushed past and tried not to think about it.

The Chinese family looked really bad. The three of them were all holding each other really tight like they didn't want to even look up, as if Porter and the old lady were still standing there. The daughter sat like a statue, and the mother clutched her hand, sniffing a lot.

Chassis was calm and quiet at the front of the bus. The wind coming through the shattered door was cold, and it was making the little pieces of glass hanging from the rubber wiggle and flap.

"Are we gonna be okay?"

"Yes," Chassis said. Rosa didn't think she meant it. She just didn't want anyone to worry.

"I'm not scared," Rosa said to her.

Chassis looked up at her for a split second before returning her gaze to the road. "Yes, you are," she said. "But you won't feel it 'til later."

Rosa didn't believe her.

"Are *you* scared?" Rosa asked her.

"You'd be crazy not to be scared," Chassis said. It wasn't a real answer. Rosa wasn't sure whether she meant she was scared or she was crazy.

"Our President will take care of us," Rosa said, over her shoulder.

Chassis looked back at her again. "You believe that?"

The question surprised Rosa. Nobody had ever asked her that before. "That's what Mamma always says," Rosa told her.

"What does it mean?" Chassis asked Rosa.

Rosa felt mad, being asked that question. Chassis *knew* what it meant. But Rosa recited what she'd learned, trying to keep from messing up. "Mamma said the market rises and falls. She says it's designed to come round again if you trust in the President. The President takes care of us. You just—"

Rosa had to stop because Chassis was snorting, looking away.

"Why you laughing?" Rosa demanded.

But Chassis didn't answer. She just shook her head and smiled the rest of her laugh away.

After a few minutes, she started looking in her side mirror. Then she kept looking in it.

"What's wrong?" Rosa asked.

At first Chassis didn't want to say. But after Rosa asked her a few more times, she finally admitted, "Someone's following us."

"It may be for our protection," she said. "But I don't like being followed." She started to speed up the bus.

She kept looking in her mirror, and it seemed like she didn't feel safe enough because she sped up again. And again.

Then they passed a sign that Rosa could see read "Ascension." "That's where our protection ends," Chassis said. As she said it, a pair of headlights came up in the side mirror like a pair of cat's eyes opening. Then another pair appeared behind it.

"They're behind us," she said. "And I think we'd better speed all the way up." She stepped on the gas hard, and the bus jerked forward.

"How fast will it go?" Rosa asked.

"I didn't want to go too fast on this road," she answered. "But if it's that or the alternative—"

"What alternative?" Rosa asked.

"You ask too many qu—" With a sickening lurch the bus leaned down, and this time everyone on the bus screamed. The bottom of the bus scraped against the road and lit up the windshield with blue sparks. Chassis pushed really hard on the brake pedal and pulled hard on the lever by her right leg. Rosa grabbed a metal bar behind Chassis' chair and hung on while her legs whipped out from under her. The air outside the windows screamed like the bus was about to flip over onto its side, but somehow Chassis hung on to the wheel and spun them right and left, and they stayed upright. Finally, they skidded to a stop.

For the first time, Chassis actually looked mad. This time she reached under her seat, and Rosa saw the revolver she didn't get a chance to pull the first time laying large in her hand. She said something into the radio and muttered at Rosa to get back to her seat.

Chassis turned back to all of them and spoke out. "Folks, this isn't good, but it's still not the end. Everyone needs to keep quiet and let me handle it."

While Chassis was talking they heard heavy footsteps on the stairs, and Porter came up with his big shotgun in his arms. But there was no old lady behind him this time. Just a bony white man with a lot of scraggly beard and a long, sharp nose.

Chassis had her gun pointed at Porter's head, right at the temple. He looked surprised, but he didn't back down or put up his hands. "You better not," he said. "You can't get back on the road without us."

"What have you done to my bus?" she asked him.

Porter grinned. His mouth was a big black hole. The man behind him said "I guess we didn't put those front tires on quite right. Your axle came right off. We can fix it back up if you want."

"Then do it," Chassis said, each word crisp like the scrape of a knife against a whetting stone.

Porter still didn't seem to care about the gun at his head. "I want something," he said to her.

"You got everything you wanted in your agreement," Chassis told him.

His cheeks puffed out. "My *Mamma* got everything!" he yelled, pouting like a child. "I didn't get *nothing* that I wanted!"

Chassis didn't react to Porter's tantrum. "You can't have anything else," she said, not backing off.

"You better put that gun down," said the man behind Porter. "Phil is standing just outside with a rifle pointed at your head."

Chassis' shoulders tensed, and then sagged, and she sat down. "You know," she said to Porter, "that the people where I come from can hear what you're saying on the radio. If you do anything—"

"I ain't gonna harm you," Porter said. "I just want what I said I want. I want the China girl for the night."

"You can't have her," Chassis said. "She's not part—"

"I want her!" Porter interrupted, spit spraying from his mouth. He moved his big belly towards Chassis. "I want her, or you ain't going anywhere! You give me that China girl..." Then he paused, and his eyes found Rosa's eyes.

Rosa tried to shrink away, but she was afraid to move. "Or I'll take that pretty little spic there." He gestured at her and took two steps down the aisle in her direction. Even though her

Mamma was all the way at the back of the bus, Rosa knew she had stopped breathing.

Instantly, all the fear she had forgotten to feel before came into her now. A sickening sense of falling with no clue as to where the bottom was. *"Daddy?"* she cried, uncertain, unable to grasp for him, unable to pull her eyes away from Porter's eyes.

But in that moment of connection between them, Porter's eyes seemed sad. He made a sound like someone was sucking the air out of his lungs, and he fell on his knees. There was a huge thump when he came down on the tilted bus floor. He was squirming, trying to get to the hole in his back where the Chinese girl's father had stuck him with a little knife, but his arms were too big and he couldn't even touch the handle. The girl's father was looking down at Porter where he had dropped, and when Porter wriggled all the way to the floor, Chassis and the man on the steps could finally see what he had done. Chassis' face got all scrunched up. "Do you know what—" she started to say as the bony-nose man practically fell down the bus stairs in his hurry to get off.

Rosa knew what was about to happen next because she was watching the Kwangs. When they got down, she got down. Then everything in the world shattered in the space of a few seconds.

After the crashing of the glass finally stopped, Rosa didn't hear any cars driving away. That's why she was scared to move. Her and everybody else. She thought the attackers were just waiting, standing around the bus with their guns pointed at the windows, ready to shoot off the first head they saw.

So nobody made a sound. She didn't know how long. All her sense of time was lost in Porter's baleful expression, painted on her mind's eye. All Rosa could think of was how sad he seemed. It confused her, that she felt bad for the man who was going to attack her.

Chassis finally rasped, "Okay. They're gone. Everybody, let me see you."

Rosa was up fast. At first, it was hard to tell who was dead and who was alive, because some people wanted to stay on the floor forever. But finally, everybody who was getting up did.

Three people stayed on the floor. First one was little Samoae. When old Mrs. Kwang saw that her baby was dead, a wail came out of her mouth. The little girl had taken a bullet through her left eye. The mama tried to hug her, but the child's body flopped around in her mother's arms. Her other eye was rolled up towards the right and her mouth was open a little. The smelly *Torture Me* Doll dropped onto the rubber mat and slid towards the front.

The Chinese man was dead, too—the father of the girl that Porter wanted. He must have been standing there when the guns were firing. He looked like such a mess Rosa couldn't have said who he was if she hadn't known. The Chinese woman and her daughter were rocking over him rhythmically, the blood leaving huge stains on their beautiful clothes.

The third person who didn't get up was Rosa's Daddy.

He was crouched down, like he had a cramp. He was breathing really hard and grinning a little. Rosa was so scared when she saw that she was afraid to run back to him. She just stood still while Mamma checked him out. Chassis slowly made her way back. The driver knelt down carefully on one knee.

"Mr. Pares," Chassis said. Her voice was tired and ragged. "Mr. Pares. Are you okay?"

"My side hurts," Rosa's Daddy said.

"Which side?"

"Left side." Then he grunted and bent over more.

"Don't move," Chassis said. "Don't move at all. Okay?"

Daddy looked like he was nodding, with his head bent down low towards the floor.

Rosa followed Chassis up to the front of the bus because Chassis was the only one who knew what was going on, and Rosa wanted to do something. The driver was moving slowly and carefully towards her seat. She stopped, and her head came over her shoulder. She didn't look at Rosa all the way, but she said, "Don't follow me. Get back there with your Daddy."

"What can I do?" Rosa asked.

"Keep your head," Chassis grunted. Then she moved forwards. Rosa went back to where her Mamma was kneeling.

"Daddy, does it hurt?" Rosa asked him into his ear. He didn't answer. "Does it hurt?" She was afraid he was already dead. Mamma tried to calm her down.

"No, baby," Daddy finally answered. It was like he was speaking up to her from the bottom of a basement stair.

Then Aunt Kin Kwang came up to Rosa's Mamma. "Our President will take care of us," she said to her.

Mamma looked up. Rosa could tell she really appreciated the comment, especially since the Kwangs had already lost their little girl. The one-eyed woman held Mamma's hand until Chassis came back.

It took longer than Rosa thought it would, but Chassis finally moved down the aisle with a box with a red letter "t" on the side. She laid it down by Rosa's Daddy, then asked him some questions, really softly.

She must have asked if he was able to move, because he finally lay on his back in the aisle. That's when Rosa saw how much blood there was. He was holding his side, and his hand was soaked. Rosa started to make a high-pitched squeal. She was embarrassed and scared at the same time.

She cried while Chassis was wrapping him up, because she couldn't do anything for him herself. Chassis worked so slowly, Rosa thought he would bleed to death before she was done. But after she finished, he did look more comfortable. His eyes were closed, and he was breathing—little shallow breaths, but regular.

"Rosa, you stay with him," Chassis said. "Doing what you're doing, letting him know he's got you." And she went back to the front of the bus, not looking to either side but keeping her head pointed at the rearview mirror. As Chassis staggered past, the Chinese woman stood up. "What do we do now?" she asked, like she was demanding a solution.

Chassis sighed and sat down heavily in her seat. She grunted as her bottom hit the chair, then her body sagged in relief.

"Ms. Chassis," the Chinese woman said, again. "What do we do now?"

Chassis didn't look at the Chinese woman. Rosa didn't know if she was mad at her for her husband having caused all of this, or what. But she kept looking out the shattered front window. "This bus will never drive again tonight," Chassis finally muttered. "Maybe—" She faded out for a second.

"Should we stay here?" asked the old man Kwang. He and his wrinkly old wife looked like they hadn't moved at all since they left port, even during the gunfire.

"Yes," Chassis rasped. "I've called into Washington. We're a little closer to them than Atlanta. They may send help."

"May?" her mother said.

Chassis didn't answer her. She just kept looking out the front window.

Nobody spoke for a little while. It was like they were waiting for Chassis to continue. But she didn't. Finally, the whispers started. Rosa wanted to talk to Chassis some more, so she got up and started walking forward.

Mamma grabbed her by the arm, yanking Rosa back. Rosa pulled free, escaped her Mama's clutching, and ignored the calls. When she got to the front of the bus, she said, "Chassis."

Chassis was sagging down in her seat like she was exhausted. She didn't look up, and she didn't answer.

Rosa didn't want to look too closely. She never saw a wound, but that didn't mean there wasn't any. She didn't know if she should tell everyone or not. Mr. Kwang noticed her standing there looking stupid. "What's wrong?" he asked, like he knew but didn't want to guess.

Rosa told him. "Chassis's dead."

Then all the whispers stopped again.

They all got off the bus and moved a little ways into the woods. Someone took Chassis' gun and gave it to the one-eyed woman to carry. They left the dead bodies on the bus where the animals wouldn't get to them. Mamma Kwang didn't want to leave Samoae, but she finally came off, sniffing, holding tight to the little maimed doll instead. *"I'll tell, I'll tell,"* the doll protested from under the fleshy part of her arm.

It was much colder out in the woods than on the bus, but at least the bugs weren't too bad. Everyone hunkered down in a big circle and just sat still, not knowing what else to do. The moonlight was blocked by the branches of the trees, so they couldn't make out anything more than the shapes of each others' bodies.

Rosa's Mamma and Mr. Kwang carried her Daddy to a flat spot and laid him down. They had wrapped him up in a blanket, but he was still moaning a little, complaining of the cold. When Rosa tried to talk to him, Mamma said to leave him alone. Suddenly angry, Rosa moved as far away from her Mamma as she could.

That put her next to Firoz. She had forgotten all about him. Through all the shooting, he had just been in the back of the bus, not moving. Rosa didn't even think he had gotten down when the guns went off. He had just sat there like it was part of the ride. The only reason he got off the bus with everyone else was because Old Lady Kwang had spent the time to try and explain to him what was going on. Rosa didn't know if the addict had even understood. But he had gotten up and followed.

They sat in the dark. At first no one said anything. Then, after a while people began speaking quietly. Mrs. Kwang asked if anyone was coming for them, and the Chinese lady said that CUSA had to honor the vouchers. Some people believed that and some people didn't. They shared a little food and the Chinese woman asked if anyone wanted to pray. They broke out the prayer arches, which were hard to see in the dark, and different people began quoting from the latest *Prospectus*, about how CUSA was just now recovering from a dip in the index and the outlook for next quarter was very positive. And everyone answered "Like, like." Rosa knew this was the kind of thing people did in emergencies, or at least she thought it was. But after a while she started getting impatient. Was sitting out here waiting to die really the only thing they could do?

She was next to Firoz, and he was the only one Rosa didn't hate right now. Because he was quiet, probably because of the stuff he had taken earlier, keeping him calm. Even though this whole situation they were in was kind of his fault, because he had tried to take drugs on the bus and her Daddy had yelled at him.

"Why do drug-worshippers take drugs anyway?" Rosa whispered to him. She thought back to the time with Basil, just a day ago and it seemed like a year. She hadn't understood then, but suddenly she wanted to understand now. Maybe it was because her parents had always kept the truth from her and here she was neck deep in reality and she didn't like that she wasn't ready.

Rosa waited a long time, but he wouldn't respond. She felt tears stinging her eyes. She wanted to talk to somebody, but even Firoz kept quiet.

Then he spoke, "The drugs require it." Rosa looked at him. At first she couldn't even believe he had answered.

"What do you mean?" Rosa asked him.

"We do what the drugs tell us," he mumbled.

"Why?" Rosa asked.

"They're trying to teach us a lesson."

"What lesson?"

"Not to use drugs," he said.

Rosa stared at him. He didn't look down at her. "I don't get it," she said.

"It's hard," he answered, nodding. Like that was an answer.

"Rosa!" her Mamma was calling. She was looking for her. Rosa was glad it was dark. She didn't want to be close to her Mamma.

Rosa was scared to death. She had never been that near to wild animals before except for squirrels and rats, never even seen any other kind except in commercials. Now everywhere she heard scratching and sniffing. She heard chattering next to her ear, and way off in the distance she heard a dog howling. At least, she assumed it was a dog. Rosa wanted to scream. Then she thought about Chassis and what she said about being scared, and she got calm again.

Her father was groaning louder now, and her Mamma bent over him. Rosa wanted to be there, too, but she didn't want to be near her Mamma. She wanted to be with her Daddy alone. Where *she* could take care of him.

It got even quieter after that, Rosa guessed, because the animals had heard the noise and stopped moving. Her Daddy kept moaning, though. Then one of the Kwang children started to whimper. She wondered if they were finally getting scared.

"We have to keep him quiet," said Mr. Kwang.

"What do you expect me to do?" demanded Rosa's Mamma.

"I don't know," said Mr. Kwang. "But if they come back—"

People were starting to argue again. Rosa noticed that praying hadn't made them feel that much better. The panic spread. Now the Chinese girl was crying, and her mother was holding her and telling her to shush.

"*You* aren't being very quiet," said Old Lady Kwang to Mr. Kwang.

"Who asked you?" said Mr. Kwang, turning to point at her with a meaty finger.

"Don't point that..." the old woman began.

Mr. Kwang didn't let her finish. "If it was me I'd have left you on the bus. Or maybe I should chase you into the woods."

"Your real mother was a hooker!" she answered him.

"Quiet!" Rosa's Mamma told them, before Mr. Kwang could push his father out of the way. "Rosa, where are you?"

"I want to pray," said Firoz, standing up. "Will anyone pray with me?"

Nobody was listening to him. That made Rosa indignant. They didn't listen to *her* either. Firoz didn't seem to care. He was fiddling around in his pouch.

"We're going to die here," the old woman said, "and I don't want to be quiet any longer. You all haven't done anything to help anyone."

"That's all you ever do!" Mr. Kwang shouted. "You complain...bitch and complain."

Mrs. Kwang said to her husband, "Stop it. This isn't—"

"Rosa!" her Mamma shouted. "Where are you?"

They were making more and more noise. But Rosa was sitting still. She was watching Firoz. He had taken out a little cigarette and was lighting it. He breathed in. The smoke curled around him and drifted away. She caught the sweet, strange scent, the one she caught at the Church, the one that was always on Basil's clothes that she knew her father would kill her for if he ever smelled it on her.

Firoz moved through all the fighting straight towards Rosa's Daddy. Nobody was paying her Daddy much attention at the moment, but now she could see that he was shivering really hard.

Rosa followed Firoz to her Daddy's side. Daddy's eyes were closed, but his head was bouncing around from side to side.

"Hold him steady," Firoz said to her. So Rosa took her Daddy's head in her hands and stroked his hair and he stopped moving enough for Firoz to stick the cigarette in Daddy's mouth. Daddy took a puff.

"*Rosa!*" her Mamma shouted. "What are you doing?" Then she gasped, as if she was unable to believe what she was seeing. "You!" She pointed a finger at the addict. She had seen Firoz giving Daddy the cigarette.

"Mamma," she said. "Wait!" She could see that Daddy wasn't shivering anymore.

"What have you done?" Rosa's Mamma screeched. "*Haven't you got any decency?*"

"I'm praying," Firoz answered.

"Get away from my husband!" She turned towards the others for help. "Get that drug filth away before I *kill* him!"

"No, Mamma, he's trying to..."

The slap Mamma gave Rosa was so swift that she was on the ground before she realized she had fallen. Through the confusion, she could still hear her Mamma shouting at Firoz.

When Rosa looked up, she saw Mamma kneeling over Daddy. "Eduardo," she said to his face.

"Pest!" Mr. Kwang said to Firoz, coming over to him. "Parasite? Why don't you leave us be?"

"You're the reason we're in this mess," said the Chinese woman, pointing a finger at the drug worshipper.

Rosa wanted to stop them. But they were rising to their feet one after the other, starting to take out their fear and anger on Firoz. One of them picked up a rock. It seemed to bounce off the drug worshipper before he knew it had hit him. He looked around suddenly, bemused, as if he had an insight. The next rock let him know what that insight was.

Stumbling to his feet, he seemed curious about all the people shouting at him, moving towards him, then scuttling away like frightened dogs. He acted like he didn't know what to do. Finally, some realization of the danger he was in dawned on him and he turned and began stumbling away.

The people followed him from the road, throwing rocks at his back until he had disappeared completely into the night. Terrified by the fury of this mob, Rosa got up and shuffled away from all the sound. Her face hurt, and she didn't understand why she felt so ashamed when she hadn't done anything wrong. She really didn't want to be around these people anymore. They were all falling apart. She wished Chassis could have been here to shut them up.

First she started walking away from the noise. And then she started running, because it felt so good to move away from all that awful yelling. She pushed through the trees and let them close behind her, to protect her from her Mamma and all those other stupid *chicopes*. But she could still hear them.

She could hear her Mamma shouting "Rosa! Rosa!" She was glad her Mamma was worried. She wasn't about to answer. She hoped her Mamma was scared shitless. She wanted her to be sorry she'd ever yelled at her daughter, much less slapped her. So she ran farther. She ran until her heartbeat was louder than the shouting.

Once she couldn't hear them anymore it occurred to her how dumb she might be acting. She considered that it was pointless to be running through the woods in the middle of the night when she didn't know where she was going. So she stopped running.

Rosa had thought that if she just turned around, she could walk back the way she came and she'd find the road again, no problem. But it didn't work out that way. For a while, she didn't hear anything. Then she made out their voices, way off in the distance.

She thought someone was calling her name. But she couldn't tell which direction the sounds were coming from. It was really hilly out there in the woods, and the hills were steep, and the noise was echoing off them. She slid down some places and then couldn't climb back up. And even when she did make it up somewhere, she only heard the sounds coming from some other direction.

She kept trying to follow the noise, but the more she wandered, the fainter they got. Rosa wanted to call out, but she was too scared about who else might hear her.

So she kept quiet and tried to listen, but the sounds got farther and farther away, and she thought she was heading in the wrong direction. She didn't know one direction from another anymore.

She wasn't sure if she was crying on purpose. She didn't remember feeling bad enough to want to die, or to stop walking, even though she was getting tired. She did remember hearing Chassis' voice in her head, telling her it was okay to be scared, and to just keep going. Keep going, the voice said.

So she kept going. And she didn't stop until she reached a clearing where the moon shone full on her. Then someone grabbed her by the shoulder and she screamed very loud.

She just knew it was Porter. She cursed in Spank, and she flailed and hit at him and scratched him with her nails. The man didn't fight back; he just kind of stood there like a tree, taking her blows, with his hand on her shoulder.

When Rosa realized it was the addict, she stopped hitting him.

"Firoz!" she said, out of breath. "Were you looking for me?"

"Hey," said Firoz, like they were old friends who had just run into each other by accident on the street.

"Hey," she gasped. His black shape looked funny through the darkness. "You know where the others are, or what?"

He seemed amazed as he looked at her. Amazed at what, she couldn't say. "Are you an angel?" he asked her. Rosa didn't understand the question until she realized that, lit up by this moon, she must look kind of ghostly. She looked at her arms and considered whether the moonlight had transformed her into a creature of light.

"I don't think so," she said.

Firoz had forgotten that he had asked the question. "I was hoping to find a Church out here," he said. "I'm out."

"What?" she demanded. "So you don't know where everybody is, either?"

"I know where everybody is," said Firoz. "But I'm out."

"Where is everybody?" Rosa asked.

"Everybody is in the future."

"In the future," Rosa repeated, looking around. She had no idea what he was talking about.

Firoz nodded. "You want to go to the future?"

"Sure, Firoz," Rosa said, losing hope again. She turned away and started walking off. Something about seeing him had made her less scared, but she wasn't exactly happy to know that he was by himself.

"The future is this way," Firoz said, and he started loping in another direction.

Rosa watched him for a second. Maybe he did know the way back. Maybe he was trying to tell her but didn't have his words all straight. Grumbling, Rosa took off after him. She figured following after him was just as good as wandering by herself, at least until she could find the voices again.

At first he seemed to know where he was going. He started moving faster up the hills than down them. Rosa tried to keep up with him as best she could, but it was hard. Her legs were sore where they were cut in a couple of places, she was starving, and she just wanted to find a warm place to lie down and go to sleep. She wished she had Basil to talk to, or somebody, or anybody.

"Hey, Firoz! Where are you headed?" she called.

He didn't answer. He didn't say anything to her at all. For a while, he was moving pretty fast in one direction. Then he started walking a more and more jagged path. Then he was making big half-circles around places where he could have gone straight. Then he stopped to look up into the trees a couple of times. When he started looping around the tree trunks, Rosa knew they were both in trouble.

"Firoz, what are you going around those trees for?"

Actually, she knew. He was messed up and didn't even understand what he was doing.

She thought about ditching him then. She thought about leaving the last grownup behind once and for all and taking her life into her own hands. But there was no way that made sense. Firoz might be crazy, but at least he was big. If they got caught by some other nasty people they might think he was protecting her.

She called out again. *"Firoz!"*

This time he stopped. He turned towards her like she had said his name for the first time. Then he sat down. He watched her as she came up to him. He was breathing heavy. "What do we do now?" he asked her.

"What?" She was astonished that he expected her to know.

He kept his eyes on her as she got real close to him, looking up at her like he was the child. His hand reached up to brush at her hair. She imagined that it was lit up by the moon like a delicate spider's web.

"Firoz, get up," Rosa said, brushing his hand away. "We have to get out of here."

Instead of getting up, he looked down and started rummaging through his pockets. He looked through each one slowly and calmly. Then he looked again. By the fourth time, he was beginning to panic.

"Can you offer me absolution?" he asked Rosa.

"No, Firoz!" she told him. "We're in the woods, you freak."

He started looking much more frantically in his pockets.

"Angel," he said to her. "Can't you tell me?"

"Firoz, we have to—"

"Tell me..." he moaned. He started to rock back and forth.

"Tell you what?" Rosa asked.

The addict looked like a little boy who has just been told he can't have a dog. He opened his mouth and began to howl. She wanted to run away from him, but he kept staring at her with big tearful eyes, and she couldn't move.

He went quiet and looked at the ground. He tried to get up. Then his legs gave way and he half-fell, half-sat. "Are you okay?" Rosa asked. She tried to pull him up. She lifted his arm, but he brushed her away.

The addict groaned and started to shiver. He wrapped his arms around himself and shook. Never taking her eyes off him, Rosa backed away and sat down too so she could lean against a tree.

Rosa decided they probably weren't going to make it.

"Where are we?"

His voice croaked out of the darkness like the cry of a deep throated frog.

"Firoz!" she answered, just because she didn't have anything else to say to him.

"Who are you?"

"I'm *Rosa*. Firoz, you *followed* me out here."

He didn't answer. She heard him grunt.

"Little boy."

"I'm *a girl!*" she shouted, and she regretted it because it echoed through the hills.

"I only need the Body and Blood," he said to his hallucination.

"I don't have any," she said.

"That's a lie," he said. "I know you have some in that bag of yours."

"You crazy," she said. She had no idea what else to tell him.

"Why do they take the Body and Blood?" he asked her, softly.

She was getting scared. It was like he was accusing her of something. Quietly, she said, "You said they take them because the drugs teach them a lesson."

Firoz's eyes opened wide. "That's right!" he said.

She hesitated because she didn't know what else he was going to say or do. When he didn't say anything, Rosa asked what she had been dying to ask him since he had told her that.

"What's the lesson?"

He answered her immediately, like he'd been waiting for the question a long time. "Drugs make everything backwards. You see from the outside looking in."

He was silent again. "That's weird," she finally said, shrugging.

"Yes," he agreed. "And it's really weird because you find out in CUSA that everything makes sense only when it's backwards." She didn't understand what that meant, but he kept talking before she could ask him another question. "The economy doesn't support us. We live to support the economy. Backwards. I find something that conflicts with what I already believe, and so I decide that it must be wrong. Backwards."

He stopped. He swallowed hard, and she saw his Adam's apple drop.

"A million people die so that I can live. Backwards."

"What are you talking about?" Rosa asked him.

"But I didn't kill a million people." He looked straight at her. "Angel? Did you hear me? I didn't kill them."

He was scaring her again. She didn't notice her own tears until they were dripping down her cheeks. "Look, Firoz," she said. "Stop, okay? We going to be okay, right?"

But he was just like all the other adults, just in his own drug way. He just kept on saying what he'd always said, only louder and louder, turning away. "Did you? Did you hear me, angel?"

"Why are you calling me that?" she demanded. She was getting tired of hearing him. Tired of looking at him, breathing in his pukey smell.

"Why do they have to die?" he wondered out loud.

"Shut *up*, Firoz!" He wasn't paying her any attention at all, really. He didn't look at her again. He didn't cock his head like he had heard her. Just said the same thing again and again, like he wanted to shout it, but was afraid.

"Tell me why!"

"Who died, Firoz?" Rosa yelled, trying to be louder than him. She wanted him to say something else, anything else.

"Why do a million people have to die?"

She didn't want to listen to him, or listen to her mother, or see her Daddy lying on the ground. She didn't want to come out here on a bus and get nearly raped by some big greasy freak. She didn't want to be in the middle of the woods with a drug addict who was coming down. She wanted to *leave*. She wanted to go home.

"It's okay, Firoz," she said to him. "Shut up!" But he had begun to shake and writhe on the ground.

His hands were on his ears. "Just tell me why!"

"Shut up, Firoz!"

"Tell me why, angel!!"

"I'll tell you, Firoz! Okay?"

"I told you to tell me why!!!"

"I'll *tell* you, Firoz, you *chicope pinga!* I'll *tell* you!" She was starting to scream through her tears, not making any sense now. She didn't know what she was going to tell Firoz. Her own voice was ragged, and it scared her how old it made her sound. That was okay. She didn't care who could hear her anymore, or what was going to happen. Porter could go ahead and do what he liked to her, because it didn't matter now. She didn't have anything left to save. "I'll tell! I'll tell!" she wailed out loud.

"You will?"

It took her a minute to hear Firoz. She was too busy wiping her eyes, coughing snot. The addict was lying on the ground, looking up at her. His gooey eyes were bloodshot, and one of them was half closed. She imagined she could see herself in the reflection of that one eye. She was amazed by her appearance, bright, shining, like she was the moon itself.

"Don't worry." The voice came from behind her. She whirled around to face the person who owned it. Her hands were clenched in tiny rock-hard fists, and she would have tried to kill the man, if she hadn't thought he was her Daddy.

He was the same height and the same shape. Rosa even said "Daddy" to him. But then she saw the gun, and she screamed.

Part Three - What Happened to Ascension

A bug crawled into her ear. She sat up panicked and pounded until it came out. She had been sleeping. Nothing was evident in the darkness in which she found herself. She had no clue to where she was. A gunshot went off somewhere far away and echoed off a hill.

When light came through the cracks in the locked door she could see that she was in a tiny room. When that door finally opened, she backed up as far from it as she could. A small, thin young woman brought her something to drink and left her without saying a word. Once again, she was left to sit alone in the dark.

Sometimes she thought she heard groaning coming from the other side of the wall. Was it a dream, or what was left over from a dream? No, because it turned to screaming. It kept on so long that she finally fell asleep to it, and then she dreamed about it.

When it was daytime, a little more light snuck in. Rosa could see whitewash over some cheap plaster that had been cracked by the incessant heat.

She could still hear his muffled screams from her little closet.

"*Qué es ese sonido?*" she asked the woman, when she came back in.

The woman shrugged. She didn't understand. She didn't speak Spanish.

"What's that sound?" she asked again in English.

"That's your father," the woman answered.

"My father?"

"The man you came here with."

"He's not my father! My father is—-"

93

The door was thrust open. A tall, haggard looking man came through and stared at her, his tortured eyes red and bloodshot. "Shut her up!" he rasped. "It's bad enough *he's* howling to wake the dead. We'll have enough of a time keeping them away."

When Rosa saw the white man, she screamed. She shoved with her feet against the floor, trying to push herself into the wall. Her hands flayed as she tried to fend off the attack she knew was coming.

"She's just a child!" snapped the woman. "What did you expect?" She put her arms around Rosa and tried to hold her still.

"Just keep her quiet!" Then he was gone back through the darkened hole, towards the howling.

Rosa's gasps subsided. She stopped trying to push away. She submitted to the woman's touch.

"Try to rest and stay quiet," said the woman, patting a little bedding on a hardwood floor. Then she left.

Rosa lay down and felt the oppressive heat smother her as the wailing went on and on. She felt something crawl across her face. She flicked it off. It hit the ground and scurried away, and she sat up quickly. Something else scuttled across her leg. She sat against the wall and kept still.

Although it got quieter, the howling didn't stop. It didn't stop during the following night, or any time during the day after that. It varied in intensity, sometimes pained, sometimes guttural. It was like a program you hadn't meant to subscribe to, one that didn't end.

Then there was something else. It came from a different direction and didn't sound like anything she'd ever heard before. It could have been commercials, but not the ones Rosa knew well, more like the one the guitar woman had played. They didn't make sense. Even through the wall, muffled, it was clear they weren't selling anything. It was just people singing, the words indistinct.

She couldn't get there to find out. She was trapped in the little closet, the door kept locked. She barely remembered being brought here now. She had no real sense of time, could have been in for one day or many days. The only way she knew it was night time was when no light came in as the woman came back to take the lamp away.

"Glory," she said. "I'm Glory." That was the white woman's name. She wasn't much bigger than Rosa, maybe not that much older. She was small and thin, with wrists not much bigger around than bones, with cheeks of the same cut. She was a strange combination of fragile and sturdy. She hadn't said much, just asked Rosa if she was hungry, brought her something to eat, some kind of flatbread, better than what Rosa usually ate, and a whole jug of water. Rosa couldn't believe how much water she was given. It smelled and tasted funny, but at least they didn't ration it out.

"You want me to bring you a book?" Glory asked. "I like to read. I have lot of books...from my father."

Rosa shook her head. There wasn't enough light to read anything that wasn't backlit. "Is that who the other man is?"

"No, he's the Pastor," she said. They sat in the closet, knees to knees, facing each other. In the dim light of the lantern her skin, riddled with bug bites and scratches, appeared dull copper, her hair thick, hardware black, long, down about to her shoulders. Her eyes in the little lamp-light were sunken.

"A drug-Padre?" She did her best with English. It was still clumsy.

"Drug?" Glory repeated, puzzled. "He's our protector, talks God to us."

"Why he keep me in the closet?"

"Nobody can know you're in here."

"Don't they hear the addict screaming?"

"Pastor told them it's my husband, that he had the fever. We live in the Fellowship hall, and that's where your friend is now while my husband is out of town."

"Everybody believes what Pastor says?"

"Sort of," Glory replied. "Pastor scares a lot of people. He has the power to scare. But everybody isn't scared of him. Not Elder Oughta. This is the kind of mistake Elder Oughta's been waiting for."

"Who's Elder Oughta?"

"The most powerful man in town. And my step-father," she remarked, though she didn't appear proud of it.

"What kind of mistake?"

Glory glared at the floor. "You," she said.

"What me?" Rosa demanded, putting her hand up to her chest. "I din' do nothing!"

"If Elder knew Pastor had taken in a couple of spiggers without telling him, he just might hang him from a tree."

Now Rosa understood. If someone would hang the Pastor, they'd do much worse to her. "How I get out of here?" she asked.

But Glory looked up, her face betraying her thoughts. "I have to go," she said.

"Wait!" Rosa said, too loud. "Don't leave me here!"

"You have to be quiet!" Glory hissed, her finger on her wide lips. "Don't you understand? Or we could all die!"

Rosa nodded, chastened. "I understand."

Glory left without another word, didn't look back. Only the click of the door was proof that she'd ever been there.

When Rosa wanted to relieve herself, she had to use a little pan in the corner. Glory took it out every few hours, but if Rosa spilled the pan at all, she had to live with the smell of anything that made it onto the floor. Even worse, the bugs seemed to gather in a more concentrated way when the waste was left for too long, and they bit more.

Eventually the stink of her own pee made her think about trying to get out of the little room. She contemplated a hundred ways to do it, to get past Glory's protesting hands, outrunning the cries of alarm. Some kind of subterfuge, persuasion, arguing. But in that last scenario, the Pastor was always behind her, huge and threatening, looking down imperious at her, his eyes blazing. "Get back in there!" he'd say.

One time Glory stayed with Rosa while she ate, and watched her.

"You're from far away," she said in a voice soft like a ruffled bedsheet. Today her thick hair was tied back with a tattered piece of blue ribbon.

"Yeah," Rosa nodded, through her food.

"What's it like?" she asked.

"I don't know!" Rosa replied. "It's my home! It's different. Where am I?"

"You're in Ascension."

"Where's that? I don't know where that is."

"About a week's walk from Richmond," she said.

Rosa shrugged. That didn't mean anything to her either.

Tell me about your home," said Glory, leaning her back against the wall and putting her arms up. "I like hearing about far away places. My mother was from somewhere far away."

"Where? CUSA?"

"Oh, no, I don't think so. Just far. She wandered in here like you did, but from some other place. The mountains, I think. I never got to ask her."

"Why?"

"She died when I was little," Glory said.

Rosa felt her eyes smart, because she wanted to ask Glory if she knew where *her* parents were. But she couldn't even bring herself to ask. She was afraid Glory wouldn't know, or worse, that she would, and that it wouldn't be good. Noticing Rosa's discomfort, Glory went on quickly. "I'll take your plate if you're done. Are you getting enough to eat?"

"When do I get out of here?" Rosa demanded.

"Sometimes I ask myself that too..." Glory answered. For a second she looked like she wanted to say more. Then some kind of sense got the better of her and she shook her head.

"I got to get back to my parents!" Rosa insisted, getting louder, because that was the only way anybody ever paid her any attention.

"Shhh!" said Glory, her eyes squinting in fright. "Look, don't shout. Wait here."

She disappeared for a minute. Rosa could hear low whispers on the other side of the door. The whispers grew more emphatic, but Rosa still couldn't hear what they were about.

At once, the door to the closet opened and closed. The Pastor loomed in the doorway. Rosa instinctively shrank back.

But the Pastor didn't threaten her. He simply stood there. He voice came out surprisingly low and quiet. "What do you want to know?"

Rosa blinked once, tried to get her equilibrium, didn't know if she could ask him. But she tried. "Are...are you going to kill me?"

"Not likely," said the Pastor gruffly. That was the extent of his answer. Rosa couldn't tell if it was sarcastic or kind.

"I have to get back...back...to my parents."

The Pastor didn't reply. He shuffled awkwardly.

"They were...on a bus with a lot of other people," Rosa said. "We had to get off the bus. I lost...I..." Her face burned. She didn't want to tell the Pastor the truth, that she ran away. "I got separated from my Mama and Daddy. I got lost in the woods."

In the dark, Rosa could see the Pastor nod once. Encouraged just a little, she went on. "I was trying to get back to them when you found me. I have to be with them to get back into CUSA. I'm from CUSA." Like he didn't know that. "They have my voucher. Without them I ain't got no *voucher*."

If the Pastor understood about vouchers, he gave no real sign. He watched her from up high, his face even more shadowed by the little light coming through the door behind him. Finally he spoke. "We're going to take care of you," he said. And that was all. He turned as though satisfied and disappeared.

Then the door closed and Rosa was alone again.

She sat there for a long time, crying, trying to understand what was happening to her. She was obviously in some small town in the Unincorporated States where she wasn't supposed to be. They had her in this closet because if anybody saw her they would do horrible stuff to her like Porter would have done.

But how long was she going to have to stay in here being eaten alive by bugs? Forever? She wasn't going to do that. Maybe there was an AVE she could use to contact her parents. They were probably looking for her, and would post in different places.

But what if her parents had never made it to DC?

Basil's face came up like he was standing in front of her. He could help. He would be able to figure something out. If she could get to an AVE.

But first she had to get out of the closet. Getting up, she moved cautiously to the locked door and turned the handle.

To her great surprise she found it was unlocked. An oversight? Glory's way of letting her out? Either way, she took the opportunity and ran. Then she was in the light, instantly relishing the air, still hot and close, but with a smell of flowers and pine. The sound of crickets just outside the window was loud as an alarm, alerting the world to her escape. The oblong space into which she had emerged was bright and silent.

It opened into a large rectangular room, a chapel with hand-carved benches going back to the door and forward to a simple raised pulpit. It looked exactly like the kind of Church that Basil worked at. A large letter "t" hung on the wall over a carpet that had once been red but now was so faded that it was practically white. The windows were open to let the musty smell escape, and when the breeze blew in she could smell the flowers from the outside.

She tiptoed up along the pews, looking left and right. There were books tucked into the pockets behind the benches, so worn and ripped that their pages would have to be held together in the hand like a bouquet of flowers.

Feeling a little braver, Rosa got down on her hands and knees behind the letter "t" display. Her eyes scanned the cardboard placard holding it in place. The whole setup was disgusting, dilapidated, and tired. Even the stains looked bored. Some small animal's droppings were barely hidden in the shadow.

Under the placard in the corner she found a small decanter. She took a sniff of something inside that she guessed was wine. She took a sip. Not too bad, actually. Sweet and musty, better than some of the stuff she'd tried at home.

She crept up and swung off the pulpit to a door along the left side. Her heart was thumping in her ears because she knew the longer she stayed out here the more likely it was someone would find her. Where was the AVE?

It took her to a hallway. At the end was a door with a sign above it that read "Fellowship Hall." The addict was in there, she knew. On the wall to the right were two doors, one of them locked.

Opening the unlocked door, she came to a little room where the Pastor kept his bed and study. On the surface of a desk lay an old book, a bible, Rosa figured out, open to something called James, the place mark resting casually over the pages. For some reason it made Rosa think of an old dirty picture she had seen once of a whore sitting with her hand draped across her thigh.

The rest of the room was plain. The little twin bed was made up neatly with a cotton blanket, a white sheet and a small pillow. Empty bookshelves sat by the bed, and a small extinguished lantern sat on a table in front of the curtained window.

It didn't even look like they had any power here, much less an AVE.

And it didn't seem like anyone was here right now either. Could she maybe look outside and see if there was power somewhere else? Well, she reasoned, it was either that or go back in the closet.

She went back to the doors at the front of the chapel and went out of them and down three uneven stone steps. Now she was in sunlight so bright it hurt. She hadn't used her eyes properly in a while. Her empty stomach was growling, and any path seemed like a good one so long as it was away from where she had been. Without a look back, she started following a thin driveway which wended into the trees.

It led to a slightly wider road, or the remains of a street. Plants had pushed through the asphalt years ago. Whole young trees straddled the remains of the painted yellow line that split it in half. She chose a direction and started walking.

It took her a second to realize that the relief she felt was from not hearing moaning and screaming anymore. She had been listening so long to it that she had filtered it out. Now that the addict was far behind her, the sound of tree branches swaying in the breeze and the chirping of insects, was blissful.

Almost instantly, the sound of talking human voices drew her on. Through the tall, solemn pines with their indifferent overcoats dropping lower and lower over her path, she ran towards that sound, knowing full well no good could come of it. She was too hungry for any kind of company now, even the wrong kind.

The bugs were as atrocious outside as they had been in the Church. No exterminators here, in the middle of the Unincorporated States. Flies, mosquitos, gnats, clouded around the thick undergrowth in the sweltering sun, and she pushed through them and their buzzing to get closer to whatever was waiting for her at the end of the path.

Something had already begun in the clearing into which Rosa peered safe from behind a tree. There was an overgrown town, green things flowing across a strip-mall of a square, and a stone building in the center where upon worn steps staggered the figure of a man outlined by the small columns running up each side.

He was short, with a shock of unwashed, dirty blond hair. His young face was lined deep with defeat, and his eyes were bloodshot. As Rosa looked more closely she saw that he was dressed in something like a sack, and that his arms and hands were clearly visible.

A heavyset, older man with a floppy, wide brimmed hat had been speaking, but his voice died down just as Rosa approached. Around him was a crowd of about fifty people. What surprised Rosa most was how dark some of them were, a couple almost as dark as her, considering that they were supposed to be whites. It may have been dirt. Some of them were absolutely speckled, their hair natty and tangled, hard to tell what color it would have been clean.

They were dressed in mean rags, their clothes either handmade and awkward, or hundred-year-old remnants of a city's throw-offs covered in grime. If Rosa had seen them in a commercial, she would have laughed, but seeing it real, there wasn't anything particularly funny about it.

Even the dog lying on the front porch looked like it was about to die in an hour.

A thin man dressed in a tattered uniform limped up to the man and stood with his back to him, facing the crowd. "Here stands Jeremiah Bloodworthy, tried and convicted by the wisdom of the Elders of the community for the crime of theft. On'y the sentence remains. Elder?" Here, the uniform nodded at the man with the hat who came to stand before Jeremiah, looking him in the eye.

"You, Jeremiah, you understand your crime?"

The accused shook his head.

"You know which commandment you have violated? Which of God's laws you have trod upon so casually?"

"Nosir," replied Jeremiah, the hopelessness rising in his face like a wave.

"Number eight," said the man. "Thou shalt not steal." He nodded once as if confirming his own words.

Jeremiah bent his head once, like the Elder had asked him to concede a point of argument.

"Standing on these here Courthouse steps, you have anything to say?"

Jeremiah raised his head. "I din't mean ta steal. Mamma," he called, looking at one remorseful grey woman in a straw hat with a plastic yellow and white daisy drooping out of it. "I'm sorry." The woman nodded, then took off her hat and hid her face in the hollow of another woman's neck.

The man with the hat stepped aside and asked, "Do the other Elders have anything to say?"

A large man with an enormous gut spoke up. "You stole from your people. You don't betray your own people, Jeremiah. Not in these times. All we got is each other. We stick together, support each other. Now we're gonna have to punish you." Jeremiah's eyes were riveted to the speaker's face as if he hoped something in the words would absolve him. But the white-haired man then glanced over at a man Rosa had seen before, the grizzled, angry Pastor.

The Pastor walked a few steps before Jeremiah, who looked searchingly at him as he approached. The Pastor came to stand directly in front of Jeremiah and put his hands gently on the sides of the man's face. Bringing his cracked lips close to Jeremiah's ear, he began to whisper something. After a second, Jeremiah nodded. The Pastor continued to whisper, and Jeremiah's eyes began to fill with tears. He whispered something back to the Pastor that Rosa really wished she could hear, and the Pastor replied quietly.

Now all of a sudden Jeremiah was openly weeping. "Please! Please help me, Pastor!"

But the Pastor had made the sign of the cross over the man, and he now backed away. "Please, Pastor!" Jeremiah cried again. "Help me!" The Pastor lowered his eyes and returned to the crowd. Now the uniform and the other men were also backing away from Jeremiah so that he stood alone upon the steps of the Courthouse.

The man in the tattered uniform came up to Jeremiah, followed by two others. They seized Jeremiah suddenly. The first man took his hand and held it out.

Rosa's body was rigid. She was certain that, should she move, they would pull her away from the trees and grab her too.

Jeremiah resisted, of course. He protested, he cried, he rocked and pulled.

The two other men held him fast. The first man in the tattered uniform pulled Jeremiah's hand out away from his body. He slowly brought it palm down upon the courthouse stairs.

The man with the large gut approached. Rosa could not see what he was carrying until he held it high, a carpenter's hammer.

Jeremiah's cries grew louder now as he looked at the stone with dread. "No! No no no!" he said, tugging and pulling against the three men who held him fast as the fat man approached.

It was over too quickly once the hammer was slammed down to its target. There was a sickening sound of bone shattering, a panicked, terrified howl, the body of the accused clenched and contracted as the three men jumped away from him.

They left him there to collapse upon the courthouse steps, alone to cradle his shattered hand in his stomach. He could barely cry out, rocked back and forth, his eyes closed.

Rosa wanted to scream. She had seen some pretty creepy things on her AVE, but the sight of Jeremiah lying on the ground with his maimed hand, no commercials cutting in, no laugh track, made her feel like it could happen to her.

Slowly the Pastor now turned, and with him turned the entire congregation of people, hat man, uniform and all, leaving Jeremiah behind. They scattered in different directions, as if the young man had been a stone they had thrown in a pond. A small group of them formed a rough line behind the Pastor and headed back up the way from which Rosa had come. She ducked behind the tree, which snagged her with its hooked bark so that she had to twist down to the ground until she could free herself. She felt vaguely like she'd lived this scene before. That's when she realized it had only probably been a week or so since she and Basil had hidden behind the gravestone, waiting to get inside the drug church. A week! Might as well have been years for all she'd seen since then.

She had a choice: Run further away, or sneak back to the church. Further away? Where? Into the *woods?* That had already gotten her lost, and she'd ended up here. The woman, Glory, would still take care of her, she thought, though she might be mad she'd gotten out. Rosa felt a sudden pang of guilt, like Glory was her mother and she'd snuck around. Impatient with her sudden rush of feelings, she focused on the train of people whom she followed, at a distance.

They headed back up the street, back through the clouds of gnats and mosquitos, and Rosa followed them, as close as she dared. She didn't swat the bugs for fear of the noise, not even as they bit her, just spat them out from time to time. The parade continued, silent all the way to the church building.

She waited until they were all inside before she dared creep in herself. Moving silently like a cat, she inched along towards the open double doors, trying hard not to be seen. She could hear a voice, harsh, rough, as if the speaker had something unpleasant in his throat that could not come up and would not go down. He talked around it, through it, and said what he had to say.

"We will all be held accountable when the clock runs out...and that time is coming soon."

Closer she crept, closer, so she could see the voice, though she knew who it belonged to. The Pastor, the man who had locked her in the closet. And sure enough, there he was, at the pulpit, preaching, while the population of Ascension sat with their backs to her in the water-stained wooden pews that creaked each time they breathed.

"Amen, Pastor," says someone. And other voices echo like water droplets. "Yes, Lord." "Amen."

Where were the drugs? Was he going to *talk* them into a stupor and then give them the fix? Rosa watched, transfixed, forgetting for a while that she was not peering into an AVE.

But another sound was competing for her attention, and was catching the ears of those in the pews as well. Rosa had to duck back as they turned around to look.

The Pastor cleared his throat, as if that would help dislodge whatever was in there, and this succeeded in getting the congregation's attention back for a moment, but the other sound was there, and it was rising, the low moan of the addict. Was that Glory speaking to him, saying "Shh shh?"

"No!" came the voice, distinct, too low to be anyone's but the addict's, and everyone turned.

"Let us look at hymn 57 in our hymnals and sing the first, second, sixth and seventh verses."

There was an instrument of some kind in the corner, leastwise that's what Rosa thought it was, since she'd never seen one except in a commercial one time, and a woman sat at it, and dropped her hands on the black and white teeth, and strange sounds came out, unearthly, guttural, like the dripping of water into a rusty jug, like the muttering of an uncertain old lady.

Behind her, someone else was playing some kind of rhythm on a homemade drum set, animal skins across some wooden frame. The beat sounded like the skeleton of some commercial she'd heard a million times. *Bummmm...bummmmmm-bummm...ba-dumm...*

She could smell the mold on the pages as they were raised from the pulpit, bird-poop-stained books with leaves that cracked under fingers. Everyone was careful, but there was no saving the books, and there would be no more books coming. Even so, they raised them and they sang, they moaned like weary travelers, they raised their noses and their voices to the ceiling and they sang.

> "*O for a thousand tongues to sing*
> *my great Redeemer's praise,*
> *the glories of my God and King,*
> *the triumphs of his grace!*"

And in the hollows of the commercial they were singing was the echoing reply of the addict from far away, moaning as if to join them in their song. "Nooooooooo," he mooed.

> *"My gracious Master and my God,*
> *assist me to proclaim,*
> *to spread through all the earth abroad*
> *the honors of thy name."*

Rosa had never heard a commercial like this. Whatever they seemed to want would not appear to them any time soon. The scene was compelling but confusing to her. The addict's cries were more insistent, and drowned out Glory's protestations into nothing. The congregation got louder too, to shut out the sound.

> *"Hear him, ye deaf; his praise, ye dumb,*
> *your loosened tongues employ;*
> *ye blind, behold your savior come,*
> *and leap, ye lame, for joy."*

From the side-door, a figure threw himself into the midst of that congregation, a man clothed only to the waist, brown wind-scarred, his arms dotted with needle punctures and scrapes, the addict, screaming, the horror of all in the room registering in shocked pale faces, jaws dropped, Glory tailing, trying to pull him back. "No! No commercials!" he cried in Spanish. "My hands! My hands! *Don't you understand?* I've tried everything!"

Weeping freely, he held his hands high to let them see the palms with the holes in them, regard how pale they were in comparison to his body and his face, to let them see that he did not belong there, was not even one of them.

The first reflex, the guns came out, revolvers, rifles, shotguns. But before they were fired, the shocked faces, the disbelief, this strange dark face in their pristine church, drips, cracked paper, and all. Then a thousand clicks of hammers and safeties.

Glory was reaching for the addict. She breathed in to cry "stop," to stay them even a second.

But Rosa was there first, inserting herself between the addict and the guns, her arms outstretched. "No! You can't! He's sick! *Stop!*"

They did stop, frozen now in a collective dumfounded stupor. The barrels of their guns wavered uncertainly, back and forth. Who would they shoot first, Rosa wondered?

"Put those guns down!" commanded the Pastor in his ragged voice. "You in God's house! Put those guns down!" He tried to recapture their attention by holding his arms out, the fingers stretched from the strain of tacking them in place. "God has no need of weapons! God will deal with these two in his own way."

"What are those animals doing here, Pastor?" asked a woman. "Why they here?"

"We found them on our doorstep!" Glory tried to explain. "In the middle of the night. We had to take them in."

Rosa looked up, surprised. She had assumed the Pastor had brought them back.

"Why?" someone demanded.

"What were we supposed to do?" Glory wheeled on them. "Leave them to the wolves? Or the maniacs in Stake's Claim?"

"Quiet, Glory," said the Pastor his voice a shade closer to soothing. And it seemed to work. The tension in the room ebbed a little, like the beginnings of a receding tidal flow. Arms stiff with guns slackened.

"Whitaker!" someone shouted out. "You knew about this?"

"Hell, no," muttered a man, coming from the back behind Glory.

"You mean, your wife hides this little girl, this maniac screams day and night, and you don't hear a thing?"

Rosa stared at the man, Whitaker. Glory had mentioned that she was married. Yet by her posture around him she gave no indication that the two of them were joined in any way.

Whitaker glared at the speaker. Whitaker was a small, severe man with a dark complexion, a boxy nose, and black hair like a bristle brush. He had a long scar deep like a river running from his eye to his upper lip. It was old, but tears or blood could have run through it and not wet the rest of the face. It made his eye baleful. "I been in Richmond these past three days working for Elder Oughta. You got a problem with my explanation?" Abruptly, he turned and glared at the assembly. No one answered him.

"I ain't putting my gun away," someone muttered.

"Well, don't then!" growled the Pastor. "But don't shoot it in here." Then he went and put his own body between Rosa and the gun barrels. He didn't look directly at her, didn't dignify her presence, just made himself a barrier between the bullet and the innocent, then shepherded her up to the pulpit.

"This is how it is," he proclaimed, turning towards them. "Jesus says we take in the poor and needy." His eyes glared low in the dim light. "You believe in Jesus, we take care of them 'til we can find a way to get them home. You don't, get out."

They murmured a little, those people, reared back in uncertainty and indecision. A tough choice.

One man spoke up. "I don't believe," he said from the back of the church. That was enough to frighten some of the people even more, and it even made Rosa uncomfortable.

"Hank," said the Pastor, "That doesn't surprise me."

It was the man in the tattered uniform. He held his gun in his arms, the barrel aimed in Firoz's general direction. "I don't believe keepin' them here is going to do any good for us. Jesus or no Jesus."

"We're gonna *keep* them?" exclaimed an elderly woman in disbelief.

"Nobody said anything about keeping them," said the Pastor, straining with discomfort.

"How we gonna take care of them? Where they gonna go?"

"Back to the woods, who cares?"

"We ain't animals," someone protested. "We don't chuck humans out to—"

"These ain't humans!" retorted Hank.

Rosa felt herself tense. She wanted to run, but the thought came to her that this was the worst thing she could do.

"What kind of garbage is that?" the Pastor demanded. "We ain't some Richmond crime ring. This is a little girl. Use your eyes, Hank."

"I'm usin' *mine,*" snarled the man who had broken Jeremiah's hand with the hammer, the man whose enormous gut now rested on his lap. "I'm usin' my eyes, and these two don't look like humans to me. They look like dirty little animals. And I know my history. They look like the end of us."

"How are they gonna be the end of us, Cob?" demanded the Pastor.

"Wake up, Pastor Harbin!" he exclaimed, leaning forward and jutting his head out. "Them and their president passed that law and kicked us out of the cities. Now they're coming to kick us out of our country."

"Right," agreed Hank. "These spiggers going to—"

"Now wait!" snapped the elderly woman. Rosa turned to look at her. The severe bones of her cheeks held steady. Rosa saw the hat in her lap, the one with the faded daisy. Rosa recognized her as Mrs. Bloodworthy, the woman whose son had been maimed. She let her rebuke ring for a second before continuing on. "I love my community and I love my people, but we can't protect anything here. Not anymore. And that ain't this little girl's fault. Nor this spegro man neither."

"They could bring trouble, but it ain't their *fault?*" Cob spoke up, making himself taller in the pews. "Well whose fault is it, then, Esther? Is it my fault? Is it your fault?"

"Well, I say maybe it's his fault!" Hank said suddenly, gesturing in Firoz's direction with the barrel of the rifle. "His and all his spigger kin. They keep us out of our cities, hold us in this miserable forest with its bugs thick as a goddamn net."

"This girl hasn't done nothing but get lost," growled the Pastor, moving a step towards Hank, his chest held high and hard. Disgruntled, Hank lowered the barrel of his rifle. "As for this man," the Pastor went on, "he's sick as a dog, attached to chemicals, the way your grandparents used to be. He don't hardly know what he's doing, he's been howling like a maniac for days."

"But why didn't you tell us the truth?" Mrs. Bloodworthy demanded.

"Look around!" the Pastor spat out. "You think you can deal with the truth, Esther? Well, okay, now you know."

Hank spoke up. "What you gonna do with them, Pastor? We got a right to—"

"Before you start tellin' me your rights," interrupted the Pastor, "You want to listen to me?"

Everyone got quiet.

"This here child was separated from her Mamma and Daddy. She may never get back to them without some kind of help. The woods are near impossible to traverse, even for our best people. We might be able to get her to Richmond with one of the food traders, but then what? Leave her there? Become some 'Bad-Old Boy' girly? You know what'll happen to her then."

Rosa didn't know exactly what would happen to her, but she had a pretty good idea. As hard as it was for her to move, she looked down at the floor. Folks noticed and they curled away in shame. The elderly woman's eyes were shining as she blinked and looked at Rosa.

"As for this man," said the Pastor, "I suppose we could get him out of here. But he's sick. All they'd do is kill him. You want to let them kill him?" The Pastor was looking at Hank. "Save them the time? Go ahead. Take him out. Kill him now."

Hank opened his mouth, then bit his lip. He looked like he couldn't decide. No one decided for him.

"All right, then," said the Pastor. "He stays. He works here until we get a better idea."

"Then you keep him *here!*" shouted uniformed Hank. "You don't let the spigger into town." A few ragged heads nodded their agreement.

"Okay," said Cob levelly. "What about the girl?"

No one answered. Rosa didn't like the silence. It was about her, but there was more to it than that, something Rosa didn't understand.

The Pastor glared at his congregants. "Nobody tells Elder Oughta about this girl. We're going to try to get her home."

They moved her to the second room on the hallway, the one which was locked. Besides a small bed, it was full of books, open and closed. The room seemed to have been occupied fairly recently but no one ever came to bother her while she was there.

Having become a resident, Rosa learned that Ascension was a town of about two hundred people, mostly subsistence farmers, men and women, who did various things besides. Elder Oughta was the town's big boss. He kept his home in a large compound a couple miles away, where he employed a number of young men, his "Gorillas," to act as peacekeepers, although they mostly guarded his compound.

She didn't see much of Ascension the first few days. Rosa mostly did chores around the Church, something she didn't particularly enjoy, but because it was with Glory, she didn't mind so much. She was told to keep inside, that she and the addict were going to lay low until someone could figure out a way to get them home.

The addict spent most of his time sitting in the little room he had been given in the Fellowship Hall as a bedroom. He ate, he slept, he moaned and sweated through his bad dreams. He sometimes walked around the Church, looking at different things, kneading his hands together to keep them from trembling. He had drunk all the wine the first time he had found it, and now the Pastor had to keep it out of sight.

She understood his need for stimulation. The only stim she had now was scratching at her bug bites. She hadn't seen an AVE in forever. Sometimes she felt like she was hallucinating. She'd hear the voice of Leethe telling her how many updates she had. She'd go to move an image and realize there was nothing in front of her.

So she took to doing chores as soon as Glory offered them to her. She had never been a fan of chores at home, not that there was ever any point to cleaning that disgusting house they lived in. But here it was chores or go crazy.

Rosa was wiping down the pews when someone opened the church door and stepped in. She peeked over the back of the pew she was kneeling on. It was Cob, with the huge, bulbous gut. He had a large lump on one side of his forehead that he fingered idly. "Look who's here," he said to her.

Rosa stayed where she was. She didn't want to approach him. She also didn't feel like she could safely move away.

Cob looked at her for a long time. "Come with me," he said suddenly.

"What?"

"The Pastor needs you in town," Cob said, arching his finger.

Rosa stared at him. "You gonna hit me with a hammer?" she demanded.

He showed her his teeth. "Not if you mind me." He turned his back and went out the door.

The air was sticky and hot, the moisture from the last storm still lingering in the tops of the trees. Rosa could barely breathe as she followed him quickly away from the house, towards the woods where the path wended to town.

Within a few minutes, they were at the strip mall and the town square, now missing Jeremiah Bloodworthy's prostrate form. People meandered to and fro across the steps where the young man had been, and didn't seem to mind that they were wandering across a grisly scene.

A few people saw Rosa, looked over at her with their bothered faces. Someone took off quickly in the direction that Rosa had come.

Cob's finger came up and pointed at the lump on his head. "You know how I got this bump?" Cob asked after a while.

Rosa shook her head.

"Bird laid a damn egg in my hair," he said, and he grinned and winked.

Rosa tried to smile too, but failed.

She followed Cob to a ladder made of steering wheels from old cars. At the top of it was a bucket on a roof.

He gestured at the ladder. "Climb up on there and get me that bucket."

She stared at him. Was he serious?

He glared back, his eyebrows coming down. "You *hear* me, girl, get up on that ladder!"

Her knees went wobbly as she moved towards the steering wheel ladder. It hung still in the heat like a dead thing.

She took a wheel in her hand, hot, plastic, smooth and gleaming in the sun. The whole rope of wheels swayed to the left. As she looked up at it she saw what she would have to do.

When she put her foot on the first wheel it protested and zipped away from her. Cob and some others nearby burst into raucous guffaws. Turning red, Rosa leapt up on it with more dexterity than any of the people behind her expected and began outclimbing her fear.

The ladder swayed ridiculously. She didn't think about that. She decided if she didn't look down, didn't stop to consider what she was doing, then she would probably make it. She was right. The wheels swayed a little less as she got higher and soon her legs were mercifully hidden from the idiots on the ground.

The bucket was waiting and she hurled it down without looking. She smirked when a voice cried out in pain, and she ducked down low behind a small retaining wall. "Come down from there!" screamed Cob. "I said come down right *now*, you spiggy bitch!" She didn't grace him with an answer.

From the roof she could see a long way off. The center of town was on a sort of ridge and the height of the building made it apparent. The trees themselves were not so tall here at the perimeter and she could see aways across the dense forest. The late afternoon sun was moving behind the undergrowth.

"What's she doing up there?" The voice of Whitaker.

"I sent her to get a bucket."

"Then you're a goddamn fool! They'll see her for sure!"

"Well, let 'em. One less mouth."

"Girly!" Whitaker demanded.

Rosa didn't answer. She peeked over until she saw the two figures, the baleful Whitaker looking up, the big buffoon Cob rubbing his head vengefully. She considered staying up there but suspected somehow that it wouldn't help. Reluctantly she swung her leg over the wall and found the ladder.

The steering wheels swung her madly away from the wall and she held on to keep from plummeting to the ground. As rapidly as she could, she lowered herself wheel by wheel, wincing at the thought of whatever Cob might be waiting to dish out to her.

"Get over here!" called Whitaker.

"She's mine!" screamed Cob, still rubbing his head. "She hit me with that bucket."

"Well why did you send her to the roof in the first place, you idiot?" Whitaker screamed.

"It was just a joke!" Cob protested. "Elder Oughta ain't in town today. He's off to Richmond."

Whitaker scowled. "Someone go get the Pastor," he shouted at a gaping onlooker. "Follow me," he growled at Rosa through his teeth.

Rosa hurried to comply. She was afraid of Cob, but she didn't know how to read Whitaker. He didn't look back at her as he took off.

The ghostly image of the town in the pale afternoon light reminded her of the closing credits of some program, frozen forever apart from the show that came before it. I know this program, Rosa thought, it's the one where the sad man gets his hand smashed by his friends.

Whitaker led her up the steps of a darkened shed. When they had entered in, he lit a couple of lanterns until the place seemed almost pleasant for a cramped, wooden room. A door led off one wall to a storage area, and another to the back stoop.

Rosa turned around fascinated. She'd never been in a place like this before. Shavings covered every surface that was not occupied by some carved thing or other, moldings, a chair, a fence post, the aroma of cut wood painted on the air of the place.

After a moment she found herself regarding the large wheel that nearly filled the room. Whitaker stood and stared at her with his hands on his hips. "Well? What you looking at?"

"What's that?"

"That's a wheel."

"I *know* it's a wheel," said Rosa, her eyebrows coming down. "I'm not *stupid*."

Whitaker didn't answer at first. He kept his hands on his hips as he glared. Finally, he said, "I got work to do."

"What's the wheel *for?*" Rosa insisted.

"To turn the lathe!" exclaimed Whitaker.

"What's a lathe?"

Whitaker threw up his hands in utter exasperation. "As if I got time to teach a blame fool everything!" He stormed a few steps off to where a cut banister lay on the floor. Quickly, he became engrossed in it and left her alone. Rosa walked over to get a closer look. "That's pretty," she said.

He looked up at her, surprised maybe that anyone besides him would think that a simple banister could be beautiful. "Go wait by the door for the Pastor," he growled, gesturing with his head. "He's comin' to get you soon."

Rosa sat on a little stool that Whitaker must have built himself. The afternoon sun waned and vanished.

On a table by the stool was a wooden carving of a rose blossom. Rosa smoothly picked it up and slipped it in her pocket where it bulged conspicuously. She looked over at Whitaker to see if he had noticed what she had done.

Whitaker had lit a lamp and continued working. He didn't seem to care about her anymore. Not sure if she should be disappointed, Rosa felt her eyes beginning to close.

"Evenin', Whitaker." It was the raggedy sound of the Pastor's voice.

Whitaker looked up with an irritated expression. "I thought you were going to keep her in the Church."

"Glory's still out of town," replied the Pastor. "And I can't do everything."

"That may be so," said Whitaker.

"We'll go, now."

Rosa was genuinely surprised that the Pastor had come for her. As a matter of course he tended to avoid her company, moving rapidly away when she was near. He seemed quiet now, as they returned up the road to the Church, and he remained a step or two ahead of her.

She tried to catch up. "Will Glory be back tomorrow?"

She saw the Pastor's right shoulder go up and down.

She came alongside him and looked up at him. He was very tall, not bent. Yet even in his strength there was a wariness, an uneasy slant to his back that might have been her and might have been more.

"Did I hear you say we were dropped off at your door?" she asked.

The Pastor tried not to look down at her. "That's so," he said.

"I don't remember that," she said.

"You were passed out cold," said the Pastor. "The other was already starting to scream again."

"So who dropped us off?"

"Someone in town, I 'spect," remarked the Pastor simply.

After a second, Rosa pressed him. "Why would they do that?"

"They probably don't want to admit they wanted to help you. They knew I would."

"Well, why did you?"

The Pastor stopped suddenly and he glared down at her. "Well, what would you have me do?" he asked. "You sorry I did?"

"No..." Rosa tried to backpedal.

"Then keep your mouth shut and stop asking questions about things we can't explain." As he moved ahead once more, she did not try to catch up again, nor ask another question.

When they reached the steps of the Church, she ran past him and went straight to her room.

"It wouldn't hurt you to sit next to him in church, at least," the Pastor put in. "Stop people talking."

"I can't help what everyone else thinks," Glory was saying. "This town is full of gossips and fools—"

Glory and the Pastor were arguing. The Wednesday service had come and gone and Rosa had passed the plate for the Pastor. Most of what she found in it were bullets.

Rosa had been dismissed to her room when it had become apparent to the adults that they were going to fight. Now the sound of their conversation came clearly through the walls, and she listened as she scratched the interminable bug bites on her arms and legs. She didn't know why they even bothered sending her away. It had become another one of the ghosts that she listened to, along with Firoz's moans and the gunshots in the distance.

"You can criticize all you want—" growled the Pastor.

"—-and murderers and—-"

"Just stop right there, before you suggest something..."

"What does he think I am?" Glory whispered.

"It's a gesture," suggested the Pastor.

"What kind of gesture, exactly?"

"I'm just sayin'—-"

Glory looked away, disgusted. "No, you're not saying anything! You've never said anything, at least not to me."

"You in a critical mood today—"

"What was that sermon about? Honoring the covenant of marriage. Who was that aimed at, exactly?"

"It's just something that needed saying..."

"Why, Pastor? Someone ain't keeping up—-"

"There's always someone ain't keeping up---"

"How do you know? Do you spy on people? Have you been checking on me? Through the keyhole?"

"You know—-"

"I don't know nothing!" Glory insisted, her voice trembling now. "If I did I wouldn't be here. I'm just one of the fools."

"What do you want to know?"

The question hung in the air. For the briefest moment, Glory sounded like she wanted to ask. But, trembling, she rose to her feet. "You'd ask me that? As if you'd ever answer!" And before the Pastor could protest, Rosa heard a sound like something striking the wall, something thrown.

Feeling in her pocket, she knew instantly what it was: the wooden rose, which she had accidentally left on the pews. Gathering up her courage, she ran out to recover it.

Glory had flown away from the front row where she and the Pastor had been sitting. The Pastor glowered sullenly, a strange, jealous look on his face. He took no notice of Rosa as she bent to find the rose.

It had been damaged by the throw. One of the petals had been broken off. Rosa didn't see it anywhere. Feeling as if she was the one who had been broken, she put the scarred rose back in her pocket.

Rosa rushed to open the door of the sanctuary. She found Glory standing there glaring out at the trees as if she didn't know which way to go. Suddenly Glory moved down the steps and stormed in a direction along the path.

Rosa crept out and began following. She thought she was being quiet, but after a minute Glory wheeled on her. "What are you doing?" she shouted.

"I don't know..." Rosa answered. "Following you?"

"Why?"

"It scared me the way you two were fighting."

Glory stared, but not at Rosa. She had cast her gaze at something just beyond Rosa's shoulder. When Rosa turned, she didn't see anything behind her, so it was clear whatever Glory was seeing was in her imagination.

Rosa turned back to Glory, whose face had softened. "Come on," she said, gesturing with her hand. "You want to take a walk?"

Rosa took Glory's hand and followed her down the main road. At some point, Glory turned right and took them on a smaller way that Rosa had never noticed. It led down a steep bank through the space between a few narrow trees.

They emerged into a bright, small clearing, well protected by the foliage. Rosa blinked in surprise. It was easily the prettiest place she'd ever seen, even in a commercial.

Glory took Rosa into the center of the clearing and they sat down in the tall grass. For a while, Glory didn't look at anything but the sky. Rosa pulled the rose from her pocket. When Glory saw it, she gave Rosa an irritated look. "Where'd you get that?" she demanded.

Instead of answering, Rosa put it back in her pocket. "Why'd you throw it?"

Glory hesitated and looked away. Rosa persisted. "Was that what you and the Pastor were arguing about?"

"Is your Mamma as pretty as you?" Glory asked.

Rosa put her hand on her chest. "Prettier," she said. "All the boys used to chase her. Was *your* Mamma pretty?"

"*Really* pretty," said Glory. "Apparently she arrived in the middle of the night and swept everybody in town off their feet. But the Elder got her. He was so in love with her that he was almost nice for a while." Glory paused and looked away.

"But he's not your daddy?"

"No," Glory shook her head.

When she didn't say anything else, Rosa asked, "Well, who *is* your father?"

"Whitaker was trying to be sweet when he made that rose for me," Glory said. "Sometimes I don't know how to take it. He's a hard man." She looked away. "And I think maybe we were married too fast."

"Why didn't you just say no?"

Glory chuckled. "When the Elder tells you you're going to marry his son—"

"His *son?*" Rosa interrupted. "Whitaker's your *brother?* You're married to—"

"Just my step-brother!" Glory said. "But yes."

Stunned, Rosa didn't say anything for a minute. She listened to the humming of the bugs. Then she asked the question she really wanted to know. "How did your Mama die?"

Glory's face paled. "Do you know how to make a daisy chain?" Deftly, she gathered together a number of small white and yellow flowers that were hiding in the grass. She beckoned to Rosa, asking her to move closer. When Rosa did, Glory turned her around. Glory pulled Rosa back by the hips so that she was sitting in her lap.

The bugs were sailing in arcs through the sunlight, lit up by every jaunt, a thousand grasshoppers and gnats sparkling on their way across the air. Even the flies looked golden in a perfect hazy afternoon. Rosa arced her head back. Glory was twisting the daisies around each other into a long chain.

"I never knew my mother," Glory said quietly from behind Rosa. "She died when I was just a baby. Well, that's what they told me."

A gunshot sounded in the distant woods.

"When I was your age," Glory went on, without stopping either her talking or her braiding, "Elder Oughta decided to give me to the Pastor. I don't know why. I think the Elder always had it in mind for me to marry Whitaker, and I guess he figured me and Whitaker should live apart until we were old enough to be together. But nobody ever talked about my Mama."

"Why not?" Rosa asked. She felt Glory attaching the daisies to her hair, weaving them in.

"She was put to death by the townspeople," Glory said, looking down.

"What did she do?"

"Mama cheated on the Elder. I think he loved her."

"Why would she do that?"

"She was angry at him, I think. Angry about something. I know she didn't come from here...she came from somewhere on the other side of the mountains...and maybe she never fit in, maybe she wanted to go back home. I'd like to go back home...where she came from. I'd like to go back across the mountains. I used to have dreams when I was little of going back and finding my mother's people, and them taking me in. I even..." She hesitated.

"What?" asked Rosa.

"Rosa, I have to ask you something."

"What?"

"There's a pattern on Firoz's shoulder. It's a bunch of blue lines."

"Really?" Rosa said, sitting up suddenly. She turned to look at Glory. "How you see that?"

"I saw it when I was...bathing him..." Glory answered, and she blushed. "What is it?"

"That his brand. He ain't supposed to have a brand, less he's somebody important in CUSA. A citizen. I don't have a brand 'cause I'm nobody."

"So he was important? Where you come from?"

"I guess so..." Rosa reached up to touch the daisies that were now entwined in her black, smooth hair.

Glory smiled. "You look pretty. Like an enchanted princess."

"Or an angel?" Rosa asked. She was wondering about Firoz. Wondering why anybody with a brand would be an addict.

Glory nodded and smiled at Rosa's question. Her face fell, and she gave Rosa an intense stare. "You won't tell anybody, won't tell him that I asked about it, will you?"

Rosa shook her head. "I can keep a secret."

Glory smiled again. "Thanks, Rosa. You're my favorite person!"

Rosa ran her fingers across the cool daisy stems that wove in and out of the strong, thick strands of her hair.

"Hey!" called a voice from the edge of the pasture.

Both of them turned. It was Whitaker, glaring from the trees.

"What are you doing, bringing her out here?"

"I do what I want," Glory said, turning away from him. She picked at the grass contemptuously.

Whitaker chewed on his lip. Glory did not turn around to face him again. Finally he snarled at Rosa, "Come with me!"

Rosa looked up at Glory. Without looking back at her, Glory shrugged.

Dutifully, Rosa got up and went over to him, leaving the sunny field behind. She thought he was going to yell at her for stealing the rose, but he didn't mention it. He turned right, towards town. They wound up back at his shop again.

When they entered the dark enclosure, he said "I got to finish this banister for some big shot in Richmond by tomorrow! You see that machine in the center of the shop?"

Rosa nodded.

"That's the lathe. This here wheel," and he gestured at the huge spoked wheel that Rosa now could not take her eyes off, "turns the lathe. At least it did, when my apprentice was here to turn it. Now I got to use this pedal." He gestured at a pedal underneath the lathe which was attached to a post by a rope.

"Can't you get a motor or something?"

Whitaker barked a laugh. "Elder Oughta keeps all the electricity for himself. He don't want us to have any power in town. We got to pay for what we use, and we don't have it to pay."

"So what happened to the apprentice?"

The question was somehow unacceptable to Whitaker. "Well!" he shouted. "When I use the pedal, I can't keep my hands still enough to do good work!" Cursing, he unhooked the hope from the pedal. Presently he had attached a new rope reaching from the wheel around and under the post. "Go on," he said, gesturing curtly. "Turn it."

"What?"

"Get over there and turn it!"

"I'm not your slave..." Rosa muttered.

"Let's go!" Whitaker ordered. Rosa, as much out of curiosity as anything else, did as she was told.

She took the handle that protruded from the wheel in both hands and turned it. The wheel obliged by making a similar circle and the rope responded, turning the post in the lathe.

"Faster," muttered Whitaker. "Faster!" he said, louder. "What's wrong? Too *hard* for you?"

Rosa had in fact just been about to complain how hard it was to turn the lathe, but Whitaker's taunt made her angry, and she found the strength. She wasn't a weakling. She had good arms.

After a second, Whitaker nodded with satisfaction. "You think you can keep that up for five minutes?"

"I can keep it up," Rosa said.

So Whitaker worked on the post, pushing into it with his tools, gradually forming a beautiful shape out of several lines. Occasionally he'd yell at Rosa to keep it *steady*, and she would curse under her breath at him. Her arms were starting to hurt, and she really needed to scratch. But she could handle it. She wasn't going to give him the satisfaction.

At last, though, she had to give up. She panted and gasped.

Whitaker's eyes bulged. "Weak! Weak, like I thought. Go on! Get out of here. Go on back to the church."

"But it's getting dark. Ain't you gonna walk me?"

Whitaker's answer was to turn her out and slam the door.

Rosa realized she had left the rose in Whitaker's shop, so she snuck back after the sun went down. The silence was stronger than she could have believed, at night in the woods. All she could hear was breathing and it almost frightened her. But it wasn't *her* breathing.

There was a sighing sound coming from inside.

No, not a sighing, too high to be a sighing, more like whining, wordless, nasal.

She wasn't used to dark like this, a complete dark, not like the brownouts in Atlanta when you didn't know what time the lights were going to come back on. This time you knew. Lights were out till morning.

Yet even in that complete darkness she could see what was on the bench by the lathe.

It was her little brother sitting there holding Samoae's *Torture Me* doll.

"Hi," he said.

"Hi," she answered.

He was the same age he was when she had last seen him, just under 8 years old. He talked more intelligently than that, though, like he was older now. "Do you know what's happened to me?" he asked.

"What do you mean?"

"Do you know where I am now?"

"You died of the toxic fever," she told him. "We couldn't afford to get your body out of cold storage for burial. We're gonna do it later. I miss you."

"How's Mamma?"

"She hasn't been nice since you died. Neither of them have. They only talk when they're fighting now. Mamma always liked you best, and Daddy liked me but he dove into the woods with a *chuseno* and I never see either of them anymore."

She snapped awake with a start and was immediately terrified because of the silence and the darkness. She didn't know where she was. She called out for her Mamma and her voice sounded tiny and thin. Then she heard the gunshot. It echoed four times off the dark hills.

She remembered where she was now. It must have been the middle of the night but she had no way to check because there weren't any clocks out here to speak of. She could still see her brother in her imagination, and she missed him because he had been right there, alive, and his words echoing through her head. *"Do you know where I am now?"* She wondered why she kept thinking about that.

Then it occurred to her what was wrong about Ascension, and what had been bothering her since she got there.

Rosa thought she could bring it up after the next Wednesday night Church service. There was a congregation meal afterwards in the Fellowship Hall, simple fare, what the people there called "seasonable vegetables." Cornbread, lemonade, fruit pies.

The meal was quieter, Glory told her, than it usually was.

Firoz had sat at the end of the table, eating like he had a hole in his side. Glory would hurry to get him as much food as she could. He didn't say thanks, and his silence, and Rosa's presence, muffled the atmosphere the way the heat did outside, put headphones over the air, hushed everything.

Rosa wondered if it was herself or the addict that was keeping everyone so silent. When people talked, it was only to their neighbors. If they wanted to speak to someone on the other side of the room they got up and walked over close to whisper. It was like listening to the AVE with the sound turned too low. It irritated her. People obviously wanted to talk louder, felt the strain of an unnatural silence, but wouldn't break it.

The addict looked as though he were in agony, wringing his hands and listing a little. He had filled out, was no longer emaciated, but the scars on his arms and the quality of the skin on his face showed the abuse of his time under the influence. When he spoke, it was halting and in a whisper. He never looked anyone in the eye, not even Rosa, and it was clear he'd rather have been back on his drugs.

Everyone else just ate. No one seemed to want to talk much. Mrs. Bloodworthy said hello to Rosa once. "How are you getting along?" she asked.

"Fine," Rosa said, looking at the floor.

Mrs. Bloodworthy bent low and whispered in her ear. "We're nice people here," she said. "You'll find out in time." Rosa thought about the hammer smashing down on her son's hand.

At the end of the meal, when everyone had gone, Rosa helped Glory clean up. Rosa waited until she was sure everyone was gone. Then she said, "I'm not the only thing they're mad about, am I?"

Glory didn't answer. She just waited. After a while, Rosa spoke again. "Where'd all the kids go?"

Glory's eyes opened wide, but it wasn't too long before she answered. "Did you ask anybody else?"

"Are they dead?" Rosa guessed.

"Good as dead, I guess," Glory said, coming towards her. Rosa started to pull away, but Glory put her arm around Rosa's shoulders and said, "You want something to eat?"

Rosa had just eaten, but the idea still sounded good.

While Glory was feeding her across a small table, she told Rosa about the other towns. "Some of them are nicer than others. Some of them are crazy. Some of them never talk to anyone else, like those people over in Stake's Claim. But those aren't the ones we worry about.

"We worry about my father, Elder Oughta. He gets us things we need, but he takes things he wants. The townspeople made deals with him, some of our Elders. Got some things we needed and hoped the weather would work out so things would grow and we could pay him back. But one year the floods didn't recede. Nothing could grow. Elder decided he had to take something." Glory stopped. She put her hand over her mouth.

Rosa wanted to ask, but she knew already. She knew the answer.

"He took the children."

"All of them," Glory went on. "From the babies to the teenagers. I was the youngest one he didn't take. Maybe because I was his."

"No," growled the Pastor from the doorway. "He was afraid a' me."

Glory smiled. "That may be true."

"An ogre, that man is, Elder Oughta," The Pastor gestured dramatically with his right arm. "If I could figure out how to bring him down, I'd do it."

"What he want them for?" Rosa asked.

"Oh, no doubt the Bad Ol' Boys in Richmond can use them..." The Pastor trailed off. He seemed unwilling to say more.

But Rosa wasn't born yesterday. She knew what grown-ups could make kids do. She'd seen some commercials she wasn't supposed to see one time, and it had given her a week of nightmares.

"That's awful."

"So they're as good as dead," Glory said quietly. "And now you're the first child in Ascension since."

"Are you and Whitaker going to have a child?"

The question embarrassed Glory greatly. She didn't even answer. The Pastor looked away, as if he wasn't sure what to say.

"Do you have sex with each other?" Rosa asked.

"*Rosa!*" Glory looked exasperated. "You can't just ask people questions like that."

In spite of himself, the Pastor grinned behind his hand.

Glory shook her head. "Whitaker wants you back at his shop this evening."

"What, again?" said Rosa.

Glory shrugged. "I guess he likes you."

"He don't like nobody!" Rosa protested.

But she went.

He hardly acknowledged her when she arrived. He had his back to her as if he was contemplating the dirt on the floor of the shop. At last he turned around.

Silently, he motioned for her to take her position at the wheel, glaring at her as she did so. When she had gotten it moving to his satisfaction, he took his position next to her and resumed his work.

She turned the wheel for him, expecting him to say something. He neither scolded her nor complimented her. Finally, when her arms were ready to burst, she stopped turning abruptly.

Whitaker's eyes bulged. Before he could say something cutting, Rosa asked abruptly, "Why did the Pastor keep us here?"

"What?" demanded Whitaker, completely taken aback.

"I mean, everybody in town hate us. We in danger just by being here. What he thinking, bringing us?"

"How the hell should I know?" Whitaker glared, throwing his arms up. He glared at the floor. "He felt sorry for you, I guess."

"So he brought us into a town where everybody hates us, where I could get killed any day? How that supposed to help us?"

Whitaker looked at her steady. "I don't know," he said. "People in this town do things for different reasons. Some of them sound nice, but not all of them are." He watched her for some sign of comprehension. Rosa squirmed, not knowing what to say. Finally, he spoke. "You take my rose?"

Rosa's mouth opened, but no sound came out. She tried to shrink into herself.

"Why'd you do that?"

Rosa shrugged.

"Come here," he said, in a tone that was a little less than an order.

Too afraid to argue, she obeyed. Walking around the lathe, she saw that he was removing the rope from the big wheel and replacing the rope from the pedal mechanism underneath. "Come around here," he instructed, "Next to me. Don't touch *nothin'* til I tell you."

Rosa nodded, silent and acquiescing.

With a few pumps of his foot, Whitaker began turning the lathe. It rotated awkwardly. "Now watch me," he said. "This here's a gouge." He held it in his hand, a silver rod with a v-shaped tip. "It's for cutting certain kinds of grooves in the wood." He gently put the gouge to the post. Immediately the wood beneath it gave, soft like it was made of clay.

"Let me try," Rosa said.

"Okay," agreed Whitaker. "But you got to do it gently. Just a touch. Like this." He touched her hand with his fingertip. "See?" He did it again.

"I see," Rosa said, nodding. "Let me try."

"Slowly," warned Whitaker.

Rosa, afraid of doing damage to the wood, advanced slowly like he said. As the tip touched the rotating post, little shavings curled away. "That's it," said Whitaker.

But her arms were still tired from her work on the wheel and she couldn't hold it steady. She gave an involuntary jerk and the gouge cleared away a chunk of the wood, temporarily stopping the wheel before it jerked forward.

"I'm sorry!" she cried. "Sorry!"

"It's okay," he said softly, patting her hand. "That's okay. It's your first time."

Rosa's neck hardened. Her breath came short. "Why you being so nice to me?" she demanded, backing away.

"What do you mean?" Whitaker said, looking mystified.

"You trying to put your hands on me?"

Whitaker's brow came down fast. "What? What are you accusing me of, girl?"

"You know what you're doing!" she yelled. "Being all mean, and now you're all nice. I know what you want!"

"You don't know nothin'!" he screamed at her, getting up suddenly. "Get out. Get out, y'damn spiggy *bitch!*"

Rosa ran without looking back, tripping down the stairs and nearly falling in the process. She heard the sound of crashing from inside the building, and it made her ashamed and afraid. She ran harder so she wouldn't have to hear it.

She pursued her fear and her anger top speed down the path, but she stopped short as she came up on the curved back of a man wearing a shirt too large for him, struggling under the weight of a large water jug on his shoulder. The loping figure didn't seem to register the sounds of Rosa's approaching feet. Nevertheless as she came up beside him, the addict, Firoz, turned slowly to the right to look at her.

"Firoz," she panted. "Hey."

The addict nodded wearily, keeping his slow, limping pace.

"Whatchu doin?" she asked him, her hands on her thighs, trying to catch her breath. She could still see Whitaker's eyes glaring down at her. She suppressed the urge to start running again.

"I'm heading towards town," he remarked, his lips making the words with difficulty, but succeeding nonetheless. His shirt was stained at the armpits. "I have to haul their water and their wood now."

"Why do you have to do that?"

Firoz shrugged. "I guess I could argue. I'm not sure that would be safe. I'm not sure what would happen."

Rosa was surprised. "You actually sound kinda normal."

"I don't know what that means anymore," Firoz remarked, shifting . "When I was taking the body and the blood, I still felt normal. Everything else was what changed. Now I'm off, I don't recognize myself. My hands hurt for no reason. I'm always hungry, and food makes me sick..."

An idea occurred to Rosa, one that she wasn't sure was the right one and that she pursued immediately. "Firoz!" she said. "Come with me."

"Where?"

"To the pasture near here. I want to get flowers."

"Flowers."

"For Whitaker," she said. "I'll tell him they're from Glory. They'll cheer him up! But I don't want to go by myself. I'm too scared. Will you come with me?"

Firoz stood uneasily like he hadn't heard the question. But he nodded once and shambled after her.

They worked their way to the pasture. As Firoz set his water jug down, Rosa ran in, delighted to see the place again. And with Firoz standing uncomfortably at the edge, looking at nothing across the fading sunlight, she felt a measure of protection, almost freedom.

"Help me find the pretty yellow ones!" she called out to Firoz.

The addict shrugged and made a half-hearted motion to come farther into the field, but he stopped short after only a single step and stood there again, swaying.

Rosa collected a bouquet of shabby golden flowers. After a while she came across a single red one, a long stem with several red florets along it. She picked it up and stuck it in the middle of the bouquet.

"What the hell you doin, spig?"

Three men stood at the edge of the field. It was Cob and Hank, and behind them was Whitaker.

Firoz looked up. "I was going into town," he muttered. "With this water. Rosa wanted to pick flowers."

"Oh, is that right?" said Cob. "You makin' us wait on our water so you can pick flowers."

Firoz eyed Cob wearily. "What do you want?"

"Just to be your friend, Seen-your." The way they said the Spanish word sounded like they were pulling a rubber band too far. "Don't you want to be friends?"

Firoz didn't answer. He stood there, staring.

"Whatcha looking at?" asked Cob again, approaching Firoz. Hank laughed. "I asked you a question. Watcha...looking...at?" Cob had his hands out in front of him and he pushed Firoz gently on the lapels. The addict, whose balance was none-too-good, staggered back.

"Hey, leave him alone," said Rosa.

Hank came into the field and grabbed Rosa behind the arms. "Let me go!" she shouted, kicking.

"The little girl-child needs to learn some manners. Don't she?" said Hank. "Don't she, Whitaker?"

Whitaker didn't answer directly. He looked away and said, "I reckon."

"Put..." Firoz managed, but before he could finish, Cob had shoved him. This time, Firoz fell back to the ground, his arms sprayed to the sides and waving like he was an overturned tortoise, disoriented.

"You'll keep silent until you're spoken to," said Cob. "And for that matter, I expect you to do your work like a good spigger and then get out of sight. Not parade about town like you're one of us. You understand?" Firoz did not answer right away. "I said, do you *understand?"* he asked again, and stepped slowly on Firoz's ribs, putting weight on the sternum. The addict grunted and gasped, finally figuring out where he was, trying to curl into a "c."

"Leave him alone!" shouted Rosa. "Leave him alone!"

"Shut the girl up," muttered Cob.

Hank grabbed her by the mouth and turned her to his face. "You gonna shut up?" he asked. "Or do I have to teach you a lesson?"

"I'll kill you, mother-*f*..." Rosa was squirming through his nasty hand.

"Huh!" said Hank, laughing. "I think I *will* have to teach her a lesson!" He seemed excited.

"Let the girl be," said Whitaker.

"What? What was that, Whitaker?" Hank called out to him, mocking. "You want me to give her to you first?"

"I said *let her be!* We came here to teach the spigger some manners, not to mess with no child."

"No child?" Hank mocked him. "Well that's a change of pace."

"What's that s'posed to mean?" Whitaker said evasively.

"Since when are you protective a kids? Time was," Hank said, "You'd have a kid in your..."

"You better shut up, Hank," Whitaker interrupted, a warning tone in his voice.

"...wood shop as your apprentice..." Hank continued, blithely.

"Shut up, Hank," Whitaker repeated, louder, aiming his face at the young man.

But Hank was laughing now. "...and you'd marry her the next month!"

Rosa felt herself shoved away. She fell back into the flowers. When she looked up, Hank and Whitaker were on one another in the tangle. Whitaker was trying to aim blows at Hank's face. Hank covered his cheeks with his forearms.

"Hey, y'all," said Cob, sticking his meaty hand out toward them. "Stop that."

"Ain't my fault!" Hank was screaming. "Get off me you half-breed..." Hank, though a little taller than Whitaker, was still unprepared and took a jab to the head. Soon he was returning a quick series of blows to Whitaker's gut. Whitaker grunted as the fists hit home, and doubled down furiously to retaliate.

"I said stop it!" yelled Cob, completely forgetting Rosa and the addict.

They were all paralyzed by the report of a gunshot. This one wasn't far off in the distance. This one was close.

Four men emerged from the woods. Each held what looked like a CUSA issued sprayer in their hands, only these weren't Young Guns. They were dressed in black shirts with matching bandanas around their heads. When Hank and Whitaker saw them, they instantly went limp and backed away. Cob stepped away from Firoz.

"Get over here," one of the men in black said to Rosa, gesturing with the barrel of his gun.

"Hey, you...you can't take her," said Whitaker. "She don't..."

"You shut up!" said the first man. "You know who we are. We take what the Elder asks for."

"But she's a child...you ain't got no..."

"Take it up with him yourself," spat the man. "I'm sure he'd be glad to talk to you about it."

Whitaker bent his head and said no more.

Rosa figured it out. These were obviously hired guns who worked for the Elder. "What do you want me for?" Rosa demanded, looking the man in the eye.

He smiled at her, an unkind, cold smile. "You're going to meet Elder Oughta!"

Thirty minutes later, she stood in front of a man who could have been a character in a commercial. He was sitting in a comfortable chair in front of a long table in the center of the expansive room. The room lay deep within the central building of a church campus that itself was larger than downtown Ascension.

The room was a kind of library or study, shelves falling down with old leatherbound books, cracked spines. But it wasn't dusty in there, Rosa noted. And a couple of the tomes were sitting on the table with pieces of paper sticking out of them.

At the moment the man wasn't interested in the books. He was absorbed in a little black checker. It was one of many pieces of plastic spread out on a patchwork of colorful boards that were arranged down the length of the table, and on others nearby. There were words on some of the boards, and line-drawn pictures in little squares, and open boxes with numbered pieces of paper, and messages on little cards, but at this angle Rosa couldn't make many of the words out.

She saw the board the Elder hovered over, nearly torn in two at the fold with age. The word *Monopoly* was still visible on its surface. Rosa knew that game. Everyone played that in elementary school. But on the AVE, not on a board.

He caught her looking, his ash-blond lashes batting across his blue eyes at regular intervals as he moved the checker forwards and back with his finger. Those eyelashes were large and soft. But there was no mistaking the clear hardness in his eyes.

When he looked up at Rosa the hardness was mitigated, just for a second, as he contemplated her. Then it returned, so fast that one could not have stopped its onslaught. He was done...he had absorbed her.

His suit also was paper white, and a felt hat lay on the table by him. From time to time he took the checker from the surface of his desk and ran it across his palm.

"Well, well, well," he finally said. She had been sitting there for five minutes. And he hadn't spoken to her in all of that time, just sat playing with the checker. "What have we here?" Did he expect her to know the answer?

"I'm Rosa." She didn't know how she dared to speak to him, only that she felt no real threat from him at the moment. He was like a snake, she decided. He would signal before he struck.

"Rosa," he said. "That's a pretty name." He looked up at her again. "And you're a pretty girl."

"Thank you," she said, simply. She'd heard that a lot lately, and it had never gone particularly well. From him, the meaning was more obscure.

"You're welcome," he answered, just as simply. Then, "Let's say you have a right to be in my town. Let's just say that."

"Your town?"

"Yes," he nodded, the ash-blond lashes nodding too. "Ascension is my town. I own it. And you're black, so you came from outside of it. But thanks to the Pastor, I hear you live there now." He took a breath. "Let's just say that's fine with me."

"You're Elder Oughta," she said.

"You've heard of me," he said.

"I heard you stole all—"

"Ho...ho...ho...hold on, now," he said, staying her with his palm. "I can't steal from my town. Please, don't insult me." He picked up the checker again from his desk and began rolling it across his palm.

"I'm sorry," Rosa said crisply. She wondered at her courage. Surely she knew how much danger she was in. But the situation seemed to call for bravado. So she went on. "All the children are gone."

"Yes," he agreed.

"They were kids!"

"Payment for a debt," he said reasonably. "The only thing they had to offer me. Anyway, not *all* the children."

Rosa swallowed.

"I heard there was a new one, a black one. And here you are."

"Here I am," she agreed, though she no longer felt so brave as she sounded. "What you gonna do about it?"

"Well, that's for me to know!" Elder Oughta said. Rubbing the checker against the side of his cheek, against his loose hanging jowls.

"How'd you get to own the town?" she found herself asking.

Elder Oughta looked pleased. He seemed to consider the question a kind of complement. "I was named after a general. Octavius was his name. Greatest of the Roman Generals. Heard of him? No, I didn't think you would. But I studied him. I decided I would be a great general, like Lincoln." Elder Oughta sighed. "But there aren't any great generals anymore. At least not on this side of the fences. So I determined to be an Elder instead, and to amass as much as I could as quickly.

"I made friends with the bosses in Richmond. They sent me men. I took this part of the country."

"That's it?" Rosa asked. She was almost disappointed.

The Elder frowned. "That's it," he said. "And why shouldn't I? I'm brighter than other people. More ambitious. Who are you?"

Rosa tried to answer, but before the sound was past her lips, he interrupted. "That's the point, isn't it? It doesn't matter who *you* are."

Rosa felt that she had to respond. Something had begun burning in her. But the Elder dismissed her with a wave. "Put the child in a locked room," he said. "Give her a bath, something to eat. I'll deal with her when I'm ready." They dragged her off, with words still trapped behind her lips and teeth.

She had gotten used to little rooms, had even grown up in them, although those she could always get out of. These more recent ones, they trapped her, trapped her in darkness. This one was more comfortable than the one before. But it was a prison nonetheless.

A man came in every few hours with some food. It was better than the food she'd been eating in the town. But somehow it didn't taste as good.

She spent a long, uncomfortable night in a hard pull-out. She noticed the bugs weren't as bad here, perhaps because the Elder could afford to spray, and this helped her to sleep. Nothing and no one bothered her until someone opened the door, lamplight pouring on her face from the hall, waking her as unmercifully as the bed had prevented her from sleeping.

"Come on out, my little mousey," said a voice she couldn't get out of her head since she'd first heard it, the gruff, eloquent voice of Elder Oughta. He was accompanied by a couple of gorillas. He paid them no mind, acted like it was just the two of them.

"Why?"

"We're going on a trip."

She complied, if only to get out of the little room. He put a proprietary hand on her shoulder as they walked down the hall. She recognized the gesture but wasn't willing to submit, rolling her shoulder out from under it.

The Elder did not condemn her rebellious attitude. He just gestured at a door. "Go in there," he said. "Take anything you want."

She almost laughed when she went in, but she was afraid of what he might do.

Dresses, beautiful blouses, pleated skirts. Girl clothes. She knew they were supposed to impress her, make her happy.

All they did was irritate her. It was so transparent. She spent twenty minutes looking at them, just to make him wait.

When she emerged, he frowned at her. She was dressed in the same clothes she'd worn going in. "I told you to get dressed," he said.

"I am dressed."

"In something nice," he retorted.

"I like what I have on."

"You'll do as you're told."

"I ain't afraid of you."

Someone slapped her with a rock-hard hand. She hadn't seen it coming. Her face twisted as she staggered and fell, thinking how she absolutely wasn't going to cry here.

The Elder stood over her. He made no move to help her up. "How about now?"

She managed to raise herself without looking him in the eye.

The Elder glared at her. "You'll put on an outfit or I'll have one of my men strip you and dress you. You *want* that?"

No, she didn't want that.

The Elder had a car. Big black car with plush seats in the back, rolling over roads that hadn't been any good in a hundred years. No doubt the Elder had someone permanent on staff to keep the vehicle fixed up.

Rosa didn't know what it ran on. It smelled like a toilet. In any case, it rolled.

They drove for several hours. The Elder didn't seem to mind that she dozed. The seats were just so comfortable and the car so quiet that she couldn't stay awake, even on the bad roads.

But when she opened her eyes a little after some indeterminate period and saw the Elder staring at her, she felt so awkward that she couldn't return to sleep, even in her exhaustion. So she looked out the window.

The scenery had changed. It was no longer forgotten country. Now there were lots of houses in rows, many in disrepair. Often she could make out aimless people sitting in front of them, the same sorts of people she saw in Atlanta all the time, numberless, useless, with nothing to do.

They overtook horse-drawn carts, one with a broken wheel sitting idle on the side of the road. The Elder's driver honked at the owner of the cart who was sitting on top of the broken wheel. He raised his hand in salute as they cruised around him without stopping.

They crossed a swollen red river into a cityscape of crumbling brick and mortar, mangled block-shaped buildings, too squat to fall over, all huddled and waiting for nothing. Some buildings had collapsed into vacant lots full of rock which dotted the landscape. Scroungers, all white people, moved across them, some of them waving at the car as they walked precariously from piece to piece of crumbled cement.

"You think I'm a monster," remarked the Elder.

Rosa shrugged and didn't look at him. She noticed something in his hands. It was the black checker, barely visible.

"I loved a dark woman once," he said.

"Where are we going?" Rosa cut in to quickly change the subject.

"Just to have a look around," replied the Elder.

"Why am I here?"

"Maybe I want to show you something."

A narrow wisp of smoke rose into the crystalline sky from a hidden, distant base, sending its message of desperation to everyone within eyeshot. It was answered by other plumes from farther out that created what looked like a sparse forest of white tree trunks in winter. The buildings that obscured the view of some of them kept silent, their eyes downcast, gazing at rubble.

Elder took Rosa into one of those buildings.

There was a smell of cooking cabbage which, while overpowering, was strangely palatable. The sound of something simmering added to the appeal of the imminent meal. As they ascended a blackened staircase they emerged on a bleached tawdry kitchen, where the back of a large woman was visible before a stove.

She turned around with a half-smile on her face, recognizing the Elder's footsteps, and she outstretched her arms "Elter!" she said, in an accent strange beyond the usual strangeness of English. Oughta moved into those arms and gave her a wet kiss upon the cheek which she accepted wholesale. "Vatchu doink here?"

"Just showing my new friend around."

The woman raised an eyebrow above her swollen, perspiring face and glanced down at Rosa. She squealed with delight and immediately assaulted the girl with a bone-crushing hug. "O, loook!" she said in her high-pitched head-voice. "She's delightful! Vere you get her? Vat's yoah name, sweet childe?"

"It's Rosa," Rosa mumbled, her mouth a short way away from the woman's ear. She smelled of scented dish soap.

"Rrrrosa," said the woman, rolling the sound in her delicious mouth. "I luf that name! You are very beautiful, Rosa!"

"Thank you."

The woman took her hand and walked her over to the stove. "Ant do you know what I am cookink?" She showed her various pots bubbling over, and pans with steaming and sizzling items.

"Not now, Vera," said the Elder. "We're here to eat, but I wanted to say hello to you before we stepped into the room."

"Okayee!" Vera nodded, and returned to her pot, dropping Rosa from her attention and focusing again on the food.

The Elder put a hand on Rosa's shoulder and steered her towards a swinging door in the opposite wall. "You like Vera?" he mumbled. "I could put you to work with her. She'd teach you a lot."

It crossed Rosa's mind faintly that she wouldn't mind that so much, but she resented the suggestion. She certainly wasn't going to give the Elder the satisfaction of seeing it. She kept her mouth shut and proceeded through the door, keeping well away from his guiding palm.

On the other side was a hushed space which was painstakingly designed to appear opulent. The room was large, almost the entire length of the building. Tall windows revealed a masterful view of the battered landscape outside, while ochre patterned curtains softened and modified it. There was something on the order of twenty large round tables arranged haphazardly in various areas of the room.

Each table was covered with linen and set with fine dishes which, if not completely free of cracks and chips, were nonetheless the finest specimens of china within a hundred metric miles. Within bowls at the center of each table were various and sundry delicacies served for the benefit of those large men who sat around each table in their long coats, skirts and trousers.

The men ate quietly. There were no women. But standing behind many of them were young people, some of whom were boys and girls around Rosa's age or a little bit older. They stood still and quiet, looking neither up nor down at the food they most likely coveted sorely, given the state of their barebones bodies, only partially covered up by the nice clothes they had been given.

The Elder took Rosa to one of the tables where two places remained empty and he invited her to sit down. She found herself surrounded by men who eyed her curiously, including one on her left side, as large as a house, who seemed to be trying not to turn and gawk at her.

"Lord, where did you get her, Oughta?" said a man from the other side of the table who was admiring her.

"Aren't you beautiful?" another asked. "What's your name?"

"Gentleman, this one's not available," said the Elder.

"What do you mean, not available?" asked a red-faced man with red hair and a wart on his nose. "What do you mean by that?"

"Only that she's not been initiated into the workings of things," replied the Elder cautiously and with courtesy. His answer failed to satisfy the man, however, who replied,

"I don't need to remind you who you work for."

"Not at all, Mister MacAllister," said the Elder, conciliatory. "Not at all. Here, now, Rosa, would you like some custard?" the Elder asked her.

Rosa didn't feel she could refuse, and it was hard not to tear into the sweet mess that was set in front of her by one of the children. She did her best to eat it slowly from the tip of the spoon. While she ate the custard, the men ate her with their eyes, until she found the sweet dessert upsetting to her stomach. But she was too hungry to push it away, so she kept going.

"Beautiful," said the man again. "Where did you get her?"

"She's an asset of Ascension."

"You do have a fine property there," replied MacAllister. "It's paid off nicely for you. Is this an offering?"

Before he would answer, the Elder tapped Rosa on the shoulder. "All right, child, run through that door and back into the kitchen. Wait for me there." As she got up, the Elder seized her arm in a tight hand and whispered in her ear, "You'd better be waiting for me when I get there, you hear me?"

Rosa nodded and made her way through the tables where other men from other parts of the room gawked and whispered to one another at her passage. Rosa kept her eyes down and hoped they couldn't see how humiliated she felt. Because now she knew. She understood.

The cook wasn't in the kitchen when she returned. Instead, several of the children were at one of the square tables eating the cabbage in plastic bowls. They were all white, mostly smaller than her, and they looked up as she entered.

She sat down next to and across from them and she smiled at them.

"You're black," one of them said to her, a little boy, about eight years old.

"That's right," she answered.

"I've never seen one of you." He stared, unabashed.

"Well, I'm not that different."

"What does it feel like to be black?"

Rosa was taken aback. "What does it feel like to be white?"

A girl answered, the one sitting next to her. "I guess it's different depending on who you are," she said.

The boy spoke up. "I wish I was white like those men out there. They're *really* white."

"What does that mean?" Rosa wanted to know.

"It means you get what you want," he said, his eyes wide.

"What do they want?"

The boy looked down and would not answer.

"Different things," said the girl quickly. "Some are easy. Some are...difficult."

"Any of you ever run away?"

"Some people run away!" said the third child, a seven-year old, excited to talk. "They never come back."

"Where do they go?"

But no one had an answer. They all looked down at their food and moved it around.

"You all live here?" Rosa asked them.

At that point the Elder came back in with Vera the cook behind. She clucked at the children for not finishing their food, touched Rosa on her head, and bustled back to the stove. The Elder put his hand on Rosa's shoulder again and Rosa, mostly to break contact, got up as quickly as she could.

The ride home in the car felt like they were returning from a funeral. The air had grown darker and the skyline had taken on a more mysterious quality. It could have been any city now, the disease and the decay disguised by the shadows and fading sunlight.

The Elder made several perfunctory remarks, presumably to get her talking. These did not work. Rosa stared out the window and tried to remember what her father's face looked like. She found that in her memory he was turning into a white man. This horrified her.

"It wouldn't be the same for you," the Elder finally said.

"What?" Rosa asked, looking up.

"You're different."

"Because I'm dark?"

"Precisely. You're a rarity out here. Most folks like you that get lost are swallowed in the hells of some of those towns out there, torn to pieces or starved to death in the woods. You had the good sense to land in my town."

"Just my luck," Rosa muttered.

"You don't know how lucky you are," exclaimed the Elder. "What a sweet life you could have here."

"What, working as the sex-slave of MacAllister?" she said, looking the Elder square in the face. He blinked several times, a reaction that looked ridiculous on him, but he held her gaze.

"We all have to make compromises," he told her. "You're obviously so smart for your age that you must know that already. You've made compromises before."

Rosa looked down. She hadn't thought so, but her memories were unreliable now.

"Well, some compromises pay off big dividends," the Elder said. "You wouldn't belong to any of them. You belong to me."

"I belong to myself!" Rosa said, angrily.

"And so..." continued the Elder, ignoring her outburst. "They can't just take you. They could, I suppose, but it would be painfully obvious what they'd done, you being impossible to hide. Then whoever did it would be the target of all the rest of them, jealous as they are, insatiable as they are."

"The bosses?"

The Elder nodded. "Yes. They work hard to keep this patchwork city from falling completely apart. They have no pleasures in life but the ones they can buy, and they guard those jealously."

"Is that where you took all the children?"

The Elder did not answer her. Without looking away, he continued, "You and I could have a very nice arrangement."

"What are you talking about? You're making me go with you. How am I going to have an arrangement with you?"

"I can compel you to do certain things," the Elder said. "I can make life very difficult for you. But that would be ruining my best asset. With your cooperation, your willing and eager cooperation, you would become much more valuable to me. I would want to treat you that much better."

"So I do what you want, eagerly and with a smile on my face, and you give me custard?"

"Don't be crass, little girl," the Elder said with a sneer. "You have no idea how rare you are, how curious these men are about you. They won't hurt you, not until they've all had a try..."

"A *try?*"

"...and by then you'll be a woman practically, and my woman at that. Don't you have any imagination at all? While you're giving them what they want, I'll be making them pay through the nose, not just money, but influence, power. And think, girl. Think of the kinds of things you could learn about them. You'll be powerful, too. You'll have power over them."

That thought set Rosa back.

For a moment, the horror of it all abated behind the notion that she could have any kind of power at all. It embarrassed her that she felt that way, wanting something so awful, and she was even more embarrassed to let the Elder see. She turned away.

"Why do you suppose the Pastor rescued you?" the Elder asked her finally.

Rosa looked at him, surprised that he would ask the same question she had asked so many times. "He said he did it for Jesus."

"Well, that's funny," said the Elder, chuckling. "Because I think he has something in mind for you, just like I do."

Rosa looked away, but the face of the Pastor came to her suddenly. It wasn't kind. Whitaker's words came into her head, then, about the reasons people did things in this town.

The Elder looked down at her like he could read her mind. "You don't know the Pastor like I do. He's not a good man. Where I'm straightforward, he keeps his devious designs to himself. Blames them on Jesus." The Elder looked out the window of the car. "He was quite happy to preside over Glory's mother's execution."

"For not wanting to sleep with you," Rosa remarked.

The Elder's cheek twitched, and he looked at her dangerously. But he made no move. "For sleeping with someone else," he said.

"How do you know?"

"Because the child wasn't mine," the Elder said. He gritted his teeth, considered, and said over lowered eyebrows, "I couldn't have..." He regrouped and began again. "I couldn't *have* a child at that time. I knew it wasn't mine. Glory was no more my daughter than you are."

Rosa stared. "Then whose daughter was she?"

"I never found out," the Elder admitted. "I could have hanged any man in town, if I'd had the notion. But she wouldn't say. And I couldn't hang them all."

He looked at her at last. "We're all evil here in Ascension," he said. "No matter what you think of your savior. What you have to do, girly, is decide who you want to trust: The one that's telling you, or the one who isn't."

"Why should I ever trust you?"

The Elder's eyebrows arched. "Who do you think rescued you?"

"What?"

"You think you turned up at the Church by accident? You think those nice boys from Stakes Claim picked you up and set you on the porch? No, child, that was my men."

Rosa was struck speechless. Her hand on her chest, she fingered the rose in her pocket. "Why would you do that?"

But Elder declined to answer. He let her alone, let her think her thoughts, as the last of the light disappeared behind the concrete blocks. When they returned to the Elder's compound, he had her escorted to her little room. They locked it and she fell upon her bed.

She screamed into the pillow so hard she thought she could tear it in two.

The Elder did not appear all day the next day. Nor did she get a chance to leave the little room. Back in her old clothes, with nothing but the wooden rose for company, she paced, looking at a couple of books she found in a drawer of a bedside table. She got meals every few hours by a gorilla that left plates and returned for them a half-hour later.

One time someone came in and stayed there while she ate, just stared at her. When she finally stared back, he didn't flinch, didn't move away, so she said, "What are you lookin' at?"

The guard didn't answer. He was small, his face completely covered by a bandana except for his eyes which watched her carefully. Rosa felt as if she'd seen those eyes before.

"Take off that bandana," she ordered, wondering at her bravery. She instantly regretted it. The man came forward towards her quickly and she knew it was all over.

As he came close, he pulled the bandana off his face.

She could only mouth his name. He grabbed her by the arm and yanked her from her seat. He put a warning hand over her mouth so that she would remember not to cry out.

You're not supposed to be here, she wanted to tell him. But Whitaker had grown up here. Was he banned since he had grown up, or did he come and go as he pleased?

He certainly seemed to know the layout. He moved her carefully down a series of halls she had not had time to memorize when she had been dragged down to the room. He seemed to be taking her somewhere in particular.

"Aren't you going to get in trouble for rescuing me?" she asked over her rapid breaths as she tried to keep up with him. He didn't answer, but only led her to a small room with no windows.

There was an AVE in it.

Rosa gasped. She ran to the AVE and it turned on as she approached, its welcoming green envelope kissing her. An Avatar appeared. "*Rosa!*" it said.

"Leethe!" Rosa cried, jumping up and down.

"*Where have you been? I have seven-thousand three-hundred and forty-two messages from your friends. Are you thirsty?*"

"Not now, Leethe. Look, I'm trying to find my parents. Are there any messages from my parents?"

"*No, Rosa.*"

Rosa bit her hand. Tears filled her eyes. She looked back at Whitaker. He still had said nothing, but was watching her balefully from the wall. "You better hurry," he muttered. "Once they know you're gone, we ain't getting out of here."

"Leethe," Rosa said, turning back towards the AVE console. "Can you find Basil? Basil Ortega, of the Drug Church at Glenwood?"

"Your friend Basil is online!" answered Leethe instantly. *"Connecting!"*

The envelope she was in wiggled once. Then Basil stood before her, looking astonished, his form blinking in the green.

"Oh Dios mio, Basil..." she said, and she started crying.

Basil reached for her, even though he knew it was silly. His hands passed through her shoulders. "Where are you? Rosa, where are you now?"

"I'm in Ascension," Rosa said, looking at the image of Basil that was wobbling severely because of the connection and the free flow of tears from her eyes. "Virgilina or something."

Basil looked to the left where a map appeared and began zeroing in. "In the US!" he exclaimed. "Crazy white people!"

"Yes!" Rosa said, and laughed through her tears.

"Are you ok?"

"There's no time for that, Basil. I lost my parents. Can you get me out of here? Can you get me home?"

"I'm just a kid, Rosa," Basil said. "I don't know how to do that!"

"But you have to, Basil! You have to do something! You said I could live with you, you said I could live at the Church! You said! You've got to, Basil, or they're going to do something awful to me, make me be a sex slave."

Basil looked sick. It seemed as though he had learned more than he wanted to know, or could handle.

"And they'll probably kill Firoz," she went on quickly.

Basil's eyes sharpened in surprise. "Who?"

"Firoz. He's an addict, Basil, from Atlanta. Do you know him?"

"His name's Firoz? Do you know anything else about him?"

"No...yes, he has a brand."

Basil got very excited. "Are you sure? Rosa are you sure his name is Firoz? Are you sure he has a brand?"

"Yes," Rosa said, nodding. "Yes, I'm sure!"

Basil started to say something, but instead vanished into blackness as the green dispersed into the corners of the room.

Rosa looked up, confused.

Whitaker was frowning. "They just cut the power. That means they know we're in here. I reckon I have about forty seconds to get you out before they corner us."

Rosa's heart was thumping madly. She felt a huge lump in her throat and stared into the empty space where Basil had been. She tried to swallow, but her chance to get home had just vanished with the green. Then panic overtook her because she remembered she wasn't just trapped in Ascension. She looked up at Whitaker. "You sure you can get us away?" Rosa asked.

Whitaker showed his yellow teeth for the first time in Rosa's memory. "It's not the first time I snuck out," he said.

He took them along a series of passages that doubled back on themselves. At one point they watched a squad of gorillas moving across a distant corridor, most likely in search of her. Finally Whitaker took them out a small service door into the woods.

Whitaker looked over at Rosa as they moved into the green. "You still crying?"

"No," Rosa snapped, wiping her eyes.

"Maybe your friend can help you."

"He just a kid. I don't even know why I asked him." Rosa looked sidewise at Whitaker, suspicious. "Why you being nice to me now?"

"I ain't being nice to you," snapped Whitaker. "The Elder likes to test people. He's let you stay in this town a long time, you and Firoz both. What I'm wondering, is that a test for you, or a test for me?"

Rosa shrugged. Whitaker shrugged too and continued, "So I figured, if it's a test for me, fuck him."

In spite of herself, Rosa laughed. She thought about the test the Elder had just given her and she thought that now maybe her and Whitaker had something in common. Running after him into the green darkness, Rosa felt a little older.

She was glad to escape the Elder's compound. But when they returned to the Pastor's small church, she was returned to prison.

Back to the little room in the Church where she had been holed up before. Only this time, no Glory to feed her. No one to tell her anything, just darkness, endless darkness and quiet, as though the Church had been shut to all comers.

She had lots of time to think, then. The AVE couldn't find her parents. They were almost certainly dead.

She cried a little. Only very softly. So no one would hear, come and see, or be angry at her for giving herself away.

Would the Pastor be willing to keep her? He had rescued her. Rosa still couldn't shake the Elder's words.

And what about the Elder? He seemed to value her. If nothing else, then for her body.

Everybody wanted her body.

She considered that one wryly as she wiped the tears away. Now that she was becoming a woman, all the wrong people were coming after her. Not the way she wanted it.

She kept these thoughts going for a long time as the darkness got deeper, as the light died from outside. Then when light came back and woke her up, she heard a rumpus in the Church, a muffled shouting that got clearer the brighter the light came. By the time it was fully day and the sun was shining under the door, she could distinguish two voices.

One was the Pastor. She recognized his harsh baritone. The other was familiar even though she didn't recognize it. Only the context of the conversation cleared it up for her.

It was the Elder.

"No, she could not have escaped by herself. It required the aid of my ridiculous son."

"I can't speak to that possibility," replied the Pastor.

"Well I can. How would you like my men to come ransack the Church until I find her?"

"I don't think the townspeople would sit idly by and let you."

A rumbling. Perhaps there were others in the sanctuary. It seemed to be getting louder.

"So it's a fight you're suggesting?"

"I'm suggesting you had no right to take this one, Elder."

"She's mine. Everything in your town is mine."

"No one's child is yours. They are all God's---"

"Spare me that garbage!" exclaimed the Elder, his contempt spilling over. "God owns me, because God can kill me. And that's why I own you."

"You didn't own our children," a woman's voice said. Mrs. Bloodworthy.

"You forfeited them when you reneged on your debt."

"How could you?"

"Woman, I do what I must do to protect this town and myself. I have debts of my own to pay."

"Where are our children?"

"God only knows," the Elder said, and his mockery was clear. The rumble of the people grew louder and indicated their feelings. "So now you will give me this last one."

"She wasn't here when you collected," said a man. Cob? "She's not part of your deal."

"She dwells here, I own her."

"What kind of arrangement is that?"

"My arrangement. If you don't like it, I can take you away too."

"What will you do, Elder?" asked the voice that must have been the Pastor's. "Take us all away?"

"If necessary."

"Then who will help you with your debts? Who will work your fields?"

"I can find idiots all over this country."

"We aren't idiots. We're the sanest town in a hundred miles, not ravaged by disease or driven mad by inbreeding. You've used us well. Don't push us too far."

"You dare? You speak to me this way? I can take away anything that you love."

"You've already taken it," interrupted the Pastor. "Not much left."

A silence that must have been the fuming of the Elder.

"What'll it be, Elder?" the Pastor continued. "A war? Don't you think injustice has its limits?"

"What do you mean?"

"The other towns, Elder. They'll find out what you've done, taken a child out of turn."

"That black child? Who loves a spigger?"

"If Elder Oughta doesn't keep his bargains, no one is safe," concluded the Pastor. "No one is safe, includes you, Elder Oughta."

"You threatening me, skirt?"

"Just pointing out the obvious. All you have, really, is guns and your good name. Give up one of them and it's that much harder to rule."

More fuming silence. More rumbling from the people. Were they gathering?

The Elder must have wondered too. "All of you going along with this madman? Do you stand against me?

"We just ask for simple justice," said Mrs. Bloodworthy, instead. "Leave the girl alone."

"That I won't do," said the Elder. More rumbling, even louder. "All right, all right," he said, reconsidering. "A bargain."

"A bargain?"

"A game."

"What kind of game?"

"The only game, of course. And the winner keeps the girl."

Rosa followed her hand past the door, into the light. She was emerging into the room before she knew it, the room with the Elder and seven of his gorillas. Her surprise was double as she saw nearly everyone she knew in the town gathered to hear the debate between the Elder and the Pastor who, seeing her, shook his head in alarm and closed his eyes.

"No," Rosa said to him. "Ain't good enough."

The Elder wheeled, almost giddy with the joy of the surprise. "Well, well!" he said. "I'd take you now, but we have a nice wager going on you and I can't bear to spoil it."

"I said ain't good enough," said Rosa.

"And what do you mean by that?" demanded the Elder, hoisting his squat body to the highest possible vantage.

"You win, you get me. I'll work with you...like you...wanted." Rosa trembled as she said it, because the Elder got that look in his eye, the look she was beginning to hate.

"Really?"

"I'll go along with it."

"Rosa, God no!" cried Glory, throwing herself up and in front of her. Rosa calmly stepped around her.

"I'll go along with it," she said again. "But if you lose..."

"Yes?"

"You find a way to get me home."

The Elder grimaced snidely. "Is that all?"

"No. You also gonna get the children of Ascension back."

Everyone in the place went silent or gasped when they heard that.

The Elder swelled. "I can't do that!" he exclaimed. "That's beyond my control."

"You got resources," Rosa said. "You'll find a way."

"I could lose a lot more than money if I did."

Rosa brought her mouth to the Elder's ear. She was so out of breath she was afraid he wouldn't be able to understand her whisper. "You'll get a lot more if you win. I won't argue with anything," she said, "I'll do it all if you're willing to...take the risk."

The Elder pulled away. He peered down at her like she was a fascinating insect. "You talk big for a little spigger girl."

She stared back without looking away. Though she trembled now and would have flinched if he'd threatened to hit her again, she looked him in the eye til he rolled his eyes in feigned disgust. "All right, burnt girl," he said. "I accept your wager. We'll play the game in seven days. Winner takes all. Don't forget your end."

"I won't."

That gave Rosa a week to learn about the game they were playing over her, the one that would decide the wager. It was an old game, like football, except that it had gone out of style in CUSA. Apparently they still played it out here, even treated it with reverence.

Rosa had never been all that interested in sports before. There were so many things to watch back home. But here it was "the only game," and learning about it kept her from feeling nauseated about what she had agreed to. As Rosa sat in church, praying with everyone else for her safe return, she began to understand that it was a game that they played when things really mattered.

And since she'd upped the ante with the Elder in front of the townspeople, everything had changed, for them, and between her and them.

She walked down the street now and she was welcomed warmly, spoken to with respect, almost as if she were an adult. Even Hank, in his ridiculous uniform, did manage a wave for her.

The young men apparently were the only ones allowed to play, and she saw them practicing off to the side, throwing their legs high as they exploded rocket throws towards one another, little white balls caught by rawhide gloves. A week. They had a week to get ready.

But they were always ready, Cob told her, sitting on the porch, his legs up over his gut, looking out at the approaching thunderclouds. He was nursing a jug of something that he'd had too much of. "Yep," he said, gently rubbing the tumor on his forehead. "It's all we got. Our respect as a town is all tied up in this here game now. Not just the game itself, mind, but the particular wager you called.

"Pastor won't tell you," he said. "But he'd love to put one over on Oughta. Ever since Glory's mother died."

Something in the way Cob spoke suggested to Rosa that he knew more than Glory had known. "How did she die?"

"Put to death in town," he remarked. "Stoned in the public square."

"That the punishment for sleeping around?"

Cob looked at her slyly. "You think you pretty smart for a girl," he said, "But no one told you the whole story, did they?"

Cob looked away. "That's 'cause it's an ugly story." He seemed to be deciding something. Finally, he opened his mouth. "Nobody wants Glory to know, least of all the Pastor. But I know...I was working for the Elder then, when I was younger, I was one of his gorillas and I saw a lot. I know things about them three that some of these here other folks don't know."

Cob rubbed his chin, considering, as if he hadn't thought about the story in a very long time. "She came to Ascension kinda like you did, from who knows where, draggled and messy. And the Pastor, he took her in just like he took you in. Well, one day the Elder caught sight of her, probably in church. And when saw her, he decided he wanted her.

"The Pastor, he always had something Elder wanted, a sort of peace of mind, or maybe a idea that he was superior to the Elder somehow. Elder wanted to take that away from the Pastor, but he never could. So he took Glory's mother instead."

Cob brought his head down, remembering more details of the story. "Well, a few months later she was with child. Only problem was, it clearly wasn't Elder's. She was too far in. So he accused her of adultery. The Pastor stood up for her, said it was the cowardly man that put her in that state should have been executed. Elder wouldn't listen. He said either the Pastor could pronounce a just sentence on his wife or he'd find something more horrible to do to her. So Pastor had to pronounce the sentence while she was pregnant, and then, after the baby was born, direct the townspeople to carry it out.

"That changed the Pastor. Elder took something from him that day, and since then Pastor's been looking for some way to get it back, or get *him* back, one or the other."

Cob nodded. "Yep," he said. "If it hadn't been you, it'd probably have been something else, eventually." Then he looked straight at her. "But I'm glad it was you."

Then the thunder roared and everyone had to go inside.

The game was scheduled for the early evening. They would all gather at the Elder's compound to eat a big meal, rest a while, and then play the game later when the heat was bearable.

That afternoon the rain came up suddenly out of what had been a clear sky, turning the earth to riddled mud in seconds. It pounded into the crowd as everyone headed for the Elder's Compound. Dripping all over the tile floors, they filed into the room that must have once been the sanctuary of the old complex. The pews had been removed long ago, and only the shape of the place, the high ceiling, the columns by the walls, provided a clue that once people worshipped here.

Rosa wasn't too happy to be back. The place stank of the few memories she had of incarceration, being held for an awful trip with awful purposes. But the whole town was present. Rosa saw Firoz being led into the hall by Glory, and Whitaker and the Pastor just behind them, and today nobody seemed to mind.

Cob held court in one corner. In another, Mrs. Bloodworthy was proudly displaying her pies, making the daisy in her hat bob with every nod, while her son sat next to her, his gnarled and crippled hand resting useless on the table. He had been sick with fever since his maiming and was only now cautiously emerging into company again.

Elder Oughta finally entered the room dressed in his white finery. The Pastor stood dutifully when he entered, and everyone followed suit. The Elder carried a rough wooden stick in one hand, and hid something in the other. He pointed the stick at individuals, who then came to him to greet him. After a while, Rosa saw that the hidden thing was the black checker which he squeezed in his palm with a compulsive motion.

After Oughta had his time, everyone was invited to sit once more. There were sweet potatoes and corn and butter beans, berry pies and slices of watermelon. In the center of the table, someone had brought a dozen scrawny chickens, courtesy of the Elder, which glistened on plates resting on the white cloth. The Pastor sat modestly along the side somewhere. The Elder took his seat at the head of the table. He raised his manicured hand for silence.

He looked around at everyone as if surveying his own family. His eyes lost focus when they come to Rosa and passed quickly over.

He rose heavily to his feet. He cleared his throat, and in his husky voice he intoned: "On September 11, 1776, our forefathers defeated the Nation of Islam in the final battle at Antietam. After the surrender of our enemy, they prayed to God and sat down together at the first Thanksgiving feast."

With practiced slowness he continued. "At that time, our nation was ruled by wise and patient men, under fear of God, and dedicated to the limitless expansion of His chosen people. We settled this land from coast to coast, from sea to shining sea. We made it beautiful.

"But over time we became careless and vain, and we forgot God and abandoned his ways. He warned us, but we heeded Him not. And so he sent the dark peoples of the earth to punish us. The black president passed a law and kicked us out. They made us into barbarians, and they sealed our cities from us."

The Elder glared. "We cannot return until God wills it, until we prove ourselves worthy, brave enough and purified enough by suffering to take what is ours.

"We are but a tenth of the men our ancestors were. Still, we are men, and still we possess our memory. For that let us say Thanks."

He looked over at the Pastor. "You want to make a prayer?" He nodded at everyone. "Join hands," he said.

Rosa found each of her hands being taken by the scarred but gentle palms of the people next to her. They bowed their heads and closed their eyes, trusting like children that she would do the same. Rosa kept her head up so she could watch.

Pastor Harbin stood in his long black robe but did not look at her. He simply opened his mouth and said, *"Now as they were eating, Jesus took bread, and blessed, and broke it, and gave it to the disciples and said, 'Take, eat; this is my body.' And he took a cup, and when he had given Thanks he gave it to them, saying, 'Drink of it, all of you; for this is my blood of the covenant, which is poured out for many for the forgiveness of sins. I tell you I shall not drink again of this fruit of the vine until that day when I drink it new with you in my Father's kingdom.'"*

Everyone nodded and replied "Amen."

Cob seemed to suddenly remember that there were two strangers at the table. He called out to Firoz, "They don't got this kind of food where you're from, do they boy? Once we left we took all the good food with us!" Everybody in the room laughed at that except Firoz, Rosa and Glory.

The addict had been in the middle of quietly deboning a breast of chicken, and looked up embarrassed, as if he had been caught stealing the food. Glory came to his rescue. "Firoz," she said, "Tell us what it's like back there now."

He looked like someone had asked him his birthday and he couldn't remember. Slowly, he spoke from a place that seemed long hidden. "Some of the commercials are nice." Nobody knew what he was talking about, but no one interrupted him. "Especially the old ones," he continued, beginning to warm to the memories. "There was one my mother used to sing me about America, when I was a boy, to get me to sleep. It was long, and she used to sing the whole thing because she liked it. She said not enough people sang the whole thing."

"Can you sing it?"

It was Hank. Rosa looked at him in surprise. He was out of his usual tatters now, dressed in the clothes he would be wearing for the game, and looked for all the world like a little kid at that moment. "I heard about America... This all used to be part of America. That's what we called it when we was all one country. Can you sing it?"

159

"*Oh, beautiful, for sacred skies,*" Firoz answered suddenly, in a surprisingly strong and lucid voice. Everyone perked up, as if they could not believe any such steadiness could come from him in any way. "*For amber waves of grain. For purple mountains majesty, above the fruited plain! America, America...*"

All of a sudden, the song seemed to hurt him. "*God mend thine every flaw...*" he tried to continue. Then he stopped.

"*God mend thine every flaw*" he began again. "*...confirm thy soul with self-control...*" he sang unsteadily, and his forehead knotted. He began to shake fully in his body. He bowed his head, embarrassed, exhausted, the effort having destroyed what he had built of his composure in that place.

There was an awkward silence.

"Cob!" Hank called out, looking across the room. "You sing *your* song!"

"Sing it!" folks started to cry in agreement, glad to break the tension.

People began whispering to themselves, then to each other. "Cob." Now louder: "Cob!" people began to say out loud, and the tumor-headed man, mangling a breastbone, looked up as if surprised, though everyone seemed to know he'd expected this.

"Sing what?" he asked through the chicken pieces. But he knew. He was already standing up to their scattered applause.

"Sing it!" everyone demanded now, in a single voice.

"All right, all right," Cob said, holding his hand out, and making a downward gesture to subdue them. He stood before his chair, resting his hand on his gut. He took a breath and his face changed. His eyes shone with joy as he sang, but the words were sad.

Sometimes I feel like a motherless child.
Sometimes I feel like a motherless child.
Sometimes I feel like a motherless child,
a long long way from home.

The townspeople fell silent as Cob sang, and they neither breathed nor scratched their arms. Even the Elder, Rosa noticed, had quieted down and remained motionless, his eyes down.

Sometimes I feel like I'm almost gone.
Sometimes I feel like I'm almost gone.
Sometimes I feel like I'm almost gone
A long, long way from home.

What did it mean?

Then others began to sing too, but they didn't sing the same song. They sang something else. It went on top of Cob's, and it fit on it funny, making a kind of a mournful, sighing combination. They sang,

Silent night,
Holy night.
All is calm, all is bright.
Round yon virgin, motherless child
Holy infant so tender and mild

And as Cob rested between verses, they finished their own.

Sleep in heavenly peace.
Sleep in heavenly peace.

Astonished, Rosa looked up at the sound of weeping, and saw that so many eyes in the hall were wet and looking at her. Some people balled up their fists and held their mouths tight, blinking rapidly as if to stem the flow. Others moaned and cried openly.

Rosa's eyes stung now, in sympathy for something she could not understand. She had heard that second commercial before, she thought. It was old. But the words seemed wrong, and she couldn't tell why.

Glory caught Rosa's attention. She seemed to have distanced herself from the emotion in the room, was using it as a distraction. As she signaled, Rosa crept over. "I need to talk to you!" Glory said quietly. "Come back to the kitchen with me?"

But they passed through the kitchen. When they moved out the back door into the rain-fresh evening, the light was still almost unbearably bright. Glory knelt down in front of Rosa. "What?" Rosa demanded.

Glory's eyes were blinking several times a second, and she seemed unable to decide what to look at. "I have to tell you," she said, in a whisper that was almost inaudible. "I need to tell you."

"What?" Rosa answered in a much louder whisper.

"Shh...shh...I need your help. I'm leaving."

"What? When?"

"Now, Rosa, during the game. It's the only time the entire town will be occupied with something, townspeople, Elder's gorillas, everyone. I'm going to make the excuse that I have to go back to the Church for a few minutes, and everyone will forget all about me. Then I can finally slip away."

"Why? Where are you going?"

"Away," Glory sighed. Her breath seemed to suggest the pathway she was going to take, invisible, a wisp that spiraled into nothing, empty air. "And I'm taking Firoz."

"Why him?"

"He told me we could go to his Church, that there are people there that could help me get across the mountains. I'm going *home.*"

"You're going to CUSA?" Rosa was breathless. "Take me with you!" Rosa demanded, pulling on Glory's arm so she bent even lower to the ground.

"I can't..." Glory said, her eyes dropping. "I can't. You have to stay here...you have to help me."

"But I want to go home!" Rosa said, her eyes pleading.

"I promise, Rosa, I promise," said Glory, "That when I get there I'll send for you. I'll send help."

"But..."

"You have to trust me, Rosa!" Glory said, her voice firm, her eyes looking steadily into Rosa's to keep her own desperation under control. "I'm in danger now if I stay. I can't say more...you don't need to know more than that. But I helped you, remember? I helped you stay alive. You have to do the same thing for me, now. I need you, Rosa. *I need you!*"

Rosa felt her face burn. "You promise? You promise you'll send help?"

"I promise," Glory nodded, taking Rosa's hands in her own. "I promise."

It could have been the worst kind of lie. Rosa had no way of knowing.

"So they don't have no Americaball in CUSA?" Mrs. Bloodworthy asked Rosa as they walked slowly through the steaming heat from the Elder's compound into the huge field behind. Her son, Jeremiah, trailed behind them, still nursing his damaged hand.

The field was full of people. It was a diamond-shape about a hundred meters on a side, and every inch of it was covered in rain-soaked lush green grass that had been cropped by some bug-eaten goats who were just now being escorted off. Gnats danced to the tune of bats cracking on the green. White blurs sailed from brown glove to brown glove and men called to one another.

"They do," Rosa said. "But it's mostly in commercials where they made it a story. I don't think they ever talk about the rules."

"The rules are easy," said Ms. Bloodworthy. "You have to get all the way around the diamond before they tag you with the ball. You have to hit it as hard as you can and then *run like hell!*" Mrs. Bloodworthy grinned. She clearly relished the game. "It's been a long time since we had a match," she said. "You've brought joy to this town, Rosa. And our boys are gonna give the Elder what's coming to him!" She gave Rosa's shoulders a squeeze. Rosa held her arm and guided her to a splintery bleacher that faced the sun.

In Ascension there were barely enough people to form a team of nine players. Still, there was something defiant today in the attitude of the young men's caps coming down over their eyes, the only occasion in which they were allowed to display such poise. The jerseys were mostly identical, sewed by someone in town, reflecting the earth, with a chalk number on the back for each of them. Jeremiah observed them miserably from beside his mother. It seemed he had once been among their number, but now would never play again.

The other team outmatched them, having nicer shirts to wear, without tatters along the bottom or threadbare holes under the arms. Their color was an angry blue, filled to overflowing with the imposing girth of the Elder's finest gorilla help. They tossed the ball with healthy contempt from hand to glove across the expectant green.

They had placed Rosa in a special seat at the front of the crowd, surrounded by a red and blue ribbon. They had allowed Mrs. Bloodworthy and Jeremiah to sit next to her just outside the ribbon, and they told her Glory would be allowed on the other side when she was finished cleaning. As the crowds gathered on both sides, Rosa saw Cob approaching the Elder. He waddled back and forth on either side of his gut until he reached the spot where the Elder sat by the dugout of the opposing team.

"What's Cob doing?" she asked Mrs. Bloodworthy.

"He's manager of this team. Used to play for the Elder when he was thinner. Long time ago. Now he'll be the one trying to beat Oughta."

"What's he saying to him?"

"They're arguing terms," Mrs. Bloodworthy explained. "He's probably telling Oughta that he wants a good, clean game. Of course Oughta will agree, but there's nothing clean about it. You can fully expect Cob will tell his men to do whatever they have to in order to survive, and Elder pulls no punches. It's part of the tradition."

As Mrs. Bloodworthy watched them, she seemed to be reading their lips or analyzing their body posture. "Now Elder is probably telling Cob what he wants and Cob can agree yes or no. There are some variations in the game and they have to negotiate."

"Can't Elder do whatever he wants?"

"He could, but it would bring him shame. The game gives Cob a chance to hold just a little power over the Elder," Mrs. Bloodworthy replied, her eyebrows high. "Just a little." Her eyes snapped back to Rosa. "Elder's playing as a wager and the game has to be tight as a drum beforehand so there's no dispute. Cob disputes, the rules get muddy, and that could end with a riot. Nobody wins then..."

Mrs. Bloodworthy squinted. "Now Cob is holding out for something...maybe an obscure rule that's to his advantage. Elder's not buying it...I think he'll give, in the end. Gets to show he's magnanimous—"

"What that mean?"

"Generous. Gracious to the little people. He likes that. It makes it seem more like he's given something up when really we're just evening the stakes."

"Are the other team that good?" Rosa asked. But Mrs. Bloodworthy didn't answer. She was staring at the two of them, her eyes now slits, her mouth a grim long line. "What is it, Mrs. Bloodworthy?"

Before the old woman could answer, a man stepped up, dressed in black with heavy padding all around him. "Teams have set terms," he called out in a voice big enough to fill the steaming greenery. Everyone fell silent to listen more attentively.

"Who's that?" Rosa whispered.

"Umpire," Mrs. Bloodworthy whispered back. "He's from Glen's Falls. That's good. He can be trusted. Elder's not taking any chances—" Whitaker turned to shush Mrs. Bloodworthy and she scowled but submitted.

"Please rise!" called the ump.

Everyone stood. An Ascension woman came out from behind the umpire, dressed in a stunning old gown. She put her hand over her heart. Following the lead of everyone in that ball park, Rosa did the same.

Then everyone shot their guns into the air.

"Play ball!" the Umpire cried. Claps turned into cheers as a young man stepped up to the plate, one of the Ascension boys.

He faced off with his bat against the pitcher, a lanky man with a greasy haircut that stuck out in feathers above his ears. The pitcher sneered left and right, surveying the field, even though there was nobody on it but his own players. He shook his head once, then shook it again. Finally he nodded, went into a crouch, raised his leg, and fired the ball at the batter.

The boy had been expecting a faster pitch and he swung too soon. The ball hit him squarely in the side and he went down. Everyone cried out, either in alarm or exultation. "Get up! Get up!" screamed Mrs. Bloodworthy while Rosa watched in wonder.

The boy, who obviously had some kind of armor on beneath his shirt, managed to get to his feet, although the ball had clearly hurt him. "He's young," muttered Mrs. Bloodworthy. "He won't make that mistake again."

The next pitch came rocketing at the boy's head, but he was watching this time. He deftly sidestepped it and brought up the bat just in time to deflect the ball. It had enough force on it to bounce significantly off the bat to the ground towards third base. Keeping the bat in his left hand, the boy ran as hard as he could towards first.

Quickly, the pitcher and first baseman converged on him. The first baseman narrowly missed having his head smashed in by the boy's bat. The pitcher decided to wait it out.

The ball, rocketed by the third baseman, sailed past the runner's shoulder, missing it by inches. The first baseman, in order to stop it, had to step off the bag, and so the boy made it safely on base.

Everyone on the town side roared at this first victory and Rosa screamed with them. The energy of a real event blew through her in a way that the sensations of the AVE never had.

The Elder looked sour but unconcerned as another young buck stepped up with his own bat.

When the ball came fast at his head, he ducked without swinging and for his cowardice received the disapproving boos of his townspeople. Cob yelled some indecipherable curse from the dugout. The Elder only smiled.

Chastened, the boy swung as hard as he could at the second pitch, but missed it by a mile. He fared no better on the third pitch. He caught the next one before it could hit him in the ribs, a feeble bunt which only flew up into the glove of the pitcher. "He'zzzout!" cried the umpire to the jeers of the Elder's team.

The runner on first, keeping the first baseman at bay with his bat, saw the next hitter and squatted low, ready to run. When that giant came out with his club, even the pitcher seemed impressed. After he made contact on the first pitch, the man on first took off at top speed.

But at the thunderous sound of a cannon he dropped flat upon his face, his free hand over his head.

"What th' hell!" screamed Cob, looking up angrily into the crowd on the Elder's side. He stomped towards the Elder. "What th' *hell!*" The ump quickly followed to intervene. "We didn't negotiate no guns!"

One of the Elder's gorillas who had been watching from the stands stood with a shotgun in his hands, pointing it in the general direction of the field. The shotgun smoked from its barrel like it was satisfied.

The Elder shrugged. "It's a home field precedent."

The Ump spoke out loud enough for everyone to hear. "Elder Oughta, did you propose guns from the audience as part of your gambit?"

"It's a home field precedent," the Elder said again. "It's something we've done in the past. The fans simply expected it."

"That's *crap!*" screamed Cob, his hands clutching his enormous hips to keep them still.

"Rules clearly stipulate no interference of any kind from the audience without a valid accord. Precedent or no precedent. Elder, you try that trick again..."

"It wasn't me!" the Elder protested, his hand on his heart. "I had nothing to do with—"

"Keep yer sneaky..."

"That's enough!" said the Ump. "We'll have to do the pitch again."

"But Shy nailed that—" Cob tried to protest.

"You want to allow the shotgun?" demanded the Ump. "I can leave it in. Your side ready to shoot?"

Cob backed down, ducking his head quickly. He stepped back to his side of the field. The owner of the shotgun grinned once and sat down, holding the gun like a teddy bear. The Ump eyed him once, and the owner of the gun stopped smiling, chastened. He put the gun on the floor of the bleachers.

Though Rosa's team showed valor, they were clearly outmatched. It was a struggle for them to keep up. In the first half inning they only scored a single run, and that at the cost of the runner's head. He was given a swift kick as he slid for home and wouldn't be able to re-emerge until the bottom of the third, with a red-splotched bandage over one eye. His absence on the field hurt the team considerably and they fell behind four runs.

Still, they gave as good as they got. At one point during the third inning, Ascension's second baseman grabbed a bat from the Elder's runner and was allowed to keep it. He decked the runner and made after the Elder's first-base hitter. Rosa watched open-mouthed as the crowd roared over the ensuing battle of bats.

The Elder's first-base hitter, a man who looked like he was made of solid iron, had only been surprised by the attack for a moment, and brought his own bat up in plenty of time. The second-baseman for Ascension tried to use his momentum to disarm the Elder's player, but the iron man stood up under the onslaught and a terrific crack could be heard all up and down the field.

The umpire watched, hawklike, for any infringement of the rules as the runner, now on the offensive, aimed a cutting blow at the second baseman's head. The town's second baseman was smaller, but nimble enough to duck and feel the breeze of the deadly swing. He came up under it and smacked the iron man in the ribs.

The crowd had remained silent since the crack of the bats, but now the Pastor stood up from his place in the crowd. He called out some unidentifiable blessing and made a gesture in the air. Heartened, the second-baseman let loose with another titanic swing.

Iron man was ready and knocked the bat clear out of his hands. The second baseman grasped for it as it flew away from him and watched it with the momentary despair of a man who knows his time has come. Smiling, the iron man reached back behind him with his own wooden weapon, his biceps bursting with veins, and prepared the killing strike.

A flash of white swallowed his face. He fell like a stone onto the ground. The town crowd cheered before Rosa saw what had happened. She looked back at the third baseman who had launched the forgotten ball directly at the iron man's face and had struck him dead in the jaw.

After a brief examination, the iron man was carried off the field. The umpire deemed him irreplaceable while the Elder screamed about rules, and so the odds were evened somewhat. Looking at the sky, the Pastor nodded and sat down.

Rosa noticed two things at once: there was still no one in the place where Glory would have sat. Whitaker rested one seat over, but Glory's chair remained conspicuously empty. She also thought she saw movement in the woods beyond the field and she knew without thinking what it was.

But the rallying cry of the crowd drowned out both thoughts. The Ascension team was out for blood now that the Elder's team had been wounded. The town's pitcher, a lanky young fellow with a twitch in his lip that did not affect his steady hand seemed determined to hold the advantage. His next three pitches were so disorienting that the Elder's batter was unable to deal with them. He swatted at the ball like it was a bee, getting out of the way to save his arms and ribs. Clearly the loss of his teammate had undermined his confidence. He was struck out without being struck.

The next hitter for the Elder fared only a little better, getting a piece of one of the pitches, but he was pegged by the ball before he reached the first base bag. Cursing, the Elder rose to his feet to chew the player out as he returned to the dugout hanging his head. The people of Ascension, sensing a rally, cheered harder and many of the neutral parties who had come to see the game began rooting for Rosa's team.

The light was fading and, as there was no practical way to light the outfield, Mrs. Bloodworthy said the game would be over when no one could see anymore, so it behooved the town to get as many runs as they could before that time. Rosa squinted into the woods as the town began to pull even with the Elder and the noise of the crowd grew.

Now a small batter from Ascension's team drew up. He had seen no success in his hitting today and he squinted as the ball came scorching towards him lit up red in the failing twilight. He didn't hit it, but he dodged it and the catcher failed to lay a glove on.

This gave the runner a chance to advance. He wasn't strong, but he was quick and in the dim light he was close to invisible. The catcher's throw missed him by a wide margin and the ball bounced up the foul line and away from first base, disappearing into the trees.

Rosa had lost track of the score, and she was too nervous to ask Mrs. Bloodworthy. It occurred to her then just what losing the game would mean, who she would be spending her time with, how they would be spending their time. No way she'd really submit to that. She'd find a way to escape.

A ludicrous idea occurred to Rosa then that maybe she should get up and go after the ball herself, maybe try to get lost in the woods again, but before she could act on it, four figures came out of the forest in the exact spot where the ball had vanished. None of them was carrying the ball.

In the gloom of the evening it was hard to see who they were against the black treeline. But as they came closer, Rosa could make out that the two on the outside were large and dressed in the black uniforms of Elder's gorillas. Then she knew without being able to see who the two people in the middle were, and she felt suddenly weak and sick.

The baseball teams slowly backed off the field. From his seat, Elder Oughta slowly stood up, his jaw set, a strange look that could have been satisfaction on his face. He gazed at the two who had been captured and taken to the pitcher's mound, left there, a little higher than everyone else, to be examined. Slowly, the people of Ascension, mixed with Elder's gorillas, came forward to surround them.

The Elder stepped before the raised mound, as if he were preparing to give a sermon. "Well," he said. "Well. Here we are, the whole family, back together."

The Pastor glared at him. "What's this about, Elder? Why have you laid hands on your daughter?"

The Elder looked snidely at the Pastor. "Are we going to keep up this game, Pastor Harbin?"

"What game? Let them loose!"

"I can't do that," the Elder replied. "And neither can you." He put his hands behind his back and smiled a little. "I have to hand it to you," he said to Glory. "You found a way to satisfy the lust that your mother gave you after all."

"It had nothing to do with that!" Glory protested. "Nothing to do with lust. Firoz promised me..." She looked at him wistfully. "A way out."

"Out? Out of what? Your home? Your covenant with your husband?"

"My *husband*?" Glory shouted, suddenly. "You match me with my *brother* so that I can never have a real..."

The Elder rushed over to her. He took her by the shoulders and shook her roughly, so that Rosa could see her teeth rattle in the yellow light of the torches that were beginning to be lit. Glory's eyes rolled back in her head. Her arms came up limply to protect herself from the massive hands of the Elder as he tore her from the ground.

"Oughta! Enough! That's enough, I said!" The Pastor had come forward, had interceded himself between them. "Enough!" He got his grizzled body in between the two of them long enough for the Elder to disengage, to drop the shaken Glory on the ground by the side of the mound. She lay there dazed, unable to speak. Firoz, true to form, seemed hardly to know what was going on. He stared at the ground by her head and said nothing.

"This ain't about her," said the Pastor, "And you know it. This is all about you and me."

"About *you!* You're just like your beloved Jesus," the Elder countered, their faces inches apart. "You always think it's about you. What an example he set. What an example you set. Teaching a girl to hate her father."

"She never hated you," said the Pastor. "No more than anyone else in this town."

"Then why do this?" he cried, gesturing wildly. "Why should she leave? Did you send her away?"

"No..." Pastor Harbin said, shaking his head. "No, I never sent her away. You take care of your own, Elder, and I take care of mine."

"Take care?" Glory laughed. She looked up at the Pastor. "You married us, against my will."

"It was a lesser sin."

"Than what? Disobedience?"

"It was a lesser sin!" the Pastor yelled, insisting.

"And so it's come to this," the Elder interrupted, taking back the focus. "This woman has committed adultery with the stranger."

"You can't prove that!" exclaimed Rosa from the side. "You don't know that for sure!" She ran from her place behind the ribbon before Mrs. Bloodworthy could stop her. Shoving through the crowd, she found her way to Glory's side. Rosa helped Glory to her feet. Glory put her hand around Rosa's body and pulled her close.

"Of course I do!" said the Elder, putting his manicured hand on his chest. "She's her mother's daughter, isn't she? Incapable of fidelity. You slept with this spigger, Glory, didn't you?"

"Elder, no!" exclaimed the Pastor, visibly distraught. "There's no proof of that!"

"She won't deny it!"

"That's because she doesn't want to give you the satisfaction, you motherfucker!" Rosa yelled.

But Rosa's insults were far beneath the Elder now and he gave her no more than a reproachful flit of his eyes before continuing. "She won't deny it. She's unfaithful and a commandment breaker." He gave Pastor Harbin a meaningful look.

"Preacher, do your duty. Declare her a sinner so I can sentence her."

"I can't," the Pastor said, trembling, taking a step away from the Elder.

The Elder frowned. "You'll do it or discredit yourself! I'll take you from this town, give you to the bosses."

The Pastor trembled. "I won't," he whispered.

"So, then." The Elder smiled again, and this time there was pleasure in his smile, even triumph. "At last I know the truth."

Horrified, the Pastor stared at the Elder, his eyes wide, his face drained of color, his expression one of a man in need of mercy. He looked from one townsperson to another as if they were the bars of a prison.

Glory's attention was rapt, now.

"She's like a daughter to me, Elder," begged the Pastor quietly, almost whispering to the Elder as if no one else were there.

"Oh, please, Pastor!" said the Elder with a contemptuous wave of his hand. "Oh, *please!* This nonsense you're perpetuating! It does you more discredit than the original sin."

"What's he talkin' about, Pastor?" Whitaker wanted to know from the side, his own voice surprisingly mild.

"I don't..." the Pastor tried to say. He could not continue. "I can't..."

"Oh my God..." Glory whispered, her hand to her mouth.

The Pastor turned to her with a piteous expression on his face, though whether he felt sorry for her, or wanted pity himself, it was hard for Rosa to say.

Glory's hand was still on her mouth, and she nodded now.

"What?" Rosa demanded, looking up at her. "What's going on?"

"All these years," said the Elder. "No way to prove it. No way for me even to ask you, you always taking the high road, Jesus' way. But now I want to know. Did my wife come to you, or did you go to her?"

The Elder let the question resonate in silence. When no one else would speak, when no one would come to his rescue, the wretched Pastor finally said, "She needed shelter from you. From your brutality."

"And so she *took* shelter...in your arms!" laughed the Elder.

"But I never..." began the Pastor

"Never what?" the Elder said, his arms splayed out like a woman's legs. "Never what, Pastor? Made love to her?"

"I don't believe it, Elder!" Glory insisted from her corner. "The Pastor would never violate the sanctity of your marriage."

"Of course not," said the Elder, sounding reasonable. "That's why he's going to assist me in setting up a stoning for *my* daughter."

Tears were pouring down the Pastor's yellow cheeks. His shoulders were shaking and his old hands were trembling.

Glory looked levelly at the Elder, now. "I see," she said. "That's why you let them stay here, Rosa and Firoz. So all this would play out and you'd get your answers." The Elder looked down at Glory mildly.

"Is that why you asked him to kill my mother," Glory went on, "to see whether he'd do it, whether he'd save himself from shame, from—?" She blinked several times fast, her eyes catching on tears. A sob escaped her. "He did." She managed to go on, looking directly at the Pastor through ruined eyes. "He saved himself. But you still suspected." The Elder did not reply.

She turned and regarded Elder Oughta again, the utmost contempt in her beautiful copper face. "You're despicable."

"Says the commandment breaker," retorted the Elder. "Well, Pastor? You going to pronounce sentence on this adulterer?"

The sight of Glory's tears had pierced the Pastor. He looked down, his own eyes full of shame. "Not this time, Elder," he said. "Not without some kind of proof..."

"I did it," Glory spoke.

The Pastor cried out as if burned, stared up at her in horror.

"I did it," she said simply. "I slept with this man. I violated my marriage oath."

"That's not true!" the Pastor protested.

But Glory smiled at him, gave him a look that meant more than he had a right to ask for, and the Pastor's face whitened in astonishment. The smile made Rosa pine. It made her think about her Daddy lying on the ground.

It was the look of a girl for her father.

When the Elder saw it, his rage overflowed in him.

"Execute them!" he screamed, pointing his finger at Glory like a weapon.

Rosa looked up at Glory, astounded. Breaking free from her arms, she rushed to grab the Pastor's vein-filled hand. "You can't do that!" Rosa demanded. "You can't let them hurt Glory, just because the Elder wanted to know whose daughter she was."

The Pastor stood up slowly. "It's...it's the law..." he said.

"That's insane!" screamed Rosa. "It was bullshit the first time! What's wrong with you? Stand up to him!"

The Pastor did not answer, but he turned away.

"Her mother was an adulterer," Elder explained to Rosa. "Like Glory. The Pastor saw fit to preside over her execution..."

"Which, of course, you forced him to do!" Glory sang out, her head held high. "Or two lives would have been lost instead of one! If he'd admitted it, you'd know whose daughter I was. You'd have killed him right after her. Maybe..." She lowered it again and gazed long at the Pastor. "I don't blame you," she whispered. "I just wanted to see my father for the first time." Glory put a hand on Rosa's arm. "It's okay, Rosa," said Glory, "It's going to be okay. I'm going to see my mother now."

Firoz had been looking at the Pastor as if he was only now recognizing him. When the Pastor finally noticed, he returned the addict's gaze. "You had to make an impossible choice!" said Firoz.

"What?" the Pastor screamed vengefully at Firoz. "*Shut your mouth!*" He grabbed the addict by the lapels and threw him to the ground. "You had no business here! I never should have let you in. The very hand of Satan! Brought into my own fold!"

Firoz brought up his arms as if to shield his head from physical blows. "It's all right!" he yelled.

"What?" demanded the Pastor, barely relenting.

"*It's all right!*" Firoz shouted again. "It's all right." And the Pastor, not understanding, stood there, straddling the addict, looking down.

"Now you have to make another impossible choice," said Firoz. "I understand that." Then he said, "I absolve you." And then he whispered something to the Pastor that no one else could hear.

Astonished by what he heard, unable to reply, the Pastor fell backwards, onto his own back. He scrambled away as from an apparition. Without a word he stared around at the townspeople.

"Pastor!" Rosa cried. She had a terrible feeling of impending loss, as if the addict had said something irrevocable. "Wait!"

But he turned without hearing her, without listening to her cries for him to stay. He stumbled to his feet and started running at top speed towards the woods. Then he disappeared into the night and was lost.

Once again the people of Ascension walked the straight path to the town square. This time Rosa was forced to be part of the procession. She had to watch Glory's sunken shoulders as she was driven before them, the addict at her side. The Elder took the front, and the two gorillas not assigned to the prisoners were behind them.

Whitaker was loping next to Rosa, just to her right. She looked at him. He kept his gaze down at the ground, mired in gloomy contemplation.

"Mr. Whitaker," she whispered, thinking about the hammer and the mangled hand. He did not respond to her call, did not look up.

"Mr. Whitaker," she tried again. "You have to do something!"

"Ain't nothin' I can do," the man muttered from behind his lips.

"You can stop this. Stand up to the Elder. Save your wife!"

"Ain't nothin' I can do," he repeated, not looking her way.

"Don't you get it?" Rosa insisted, whispering fiercely. "You're part of this! He wants you to suffer too!"

But Whitaker had no answer. The lit up town square was coming into view.

The people had gathered around the courthouse steps. They had been waiting for the Elder's gorillas to bring Glory and Firoz to be judged in a circle of torchlight that barely lit up the edge of the trees. Rosa had been dragged along and left to stand by Mrs. Bloodworthy whose maimed son, Jeremiah, cowered behind her, still afraid of the spectacle.

Cob loped forward, facing the crowd. "Here stands Glory Oughta who has been tried and convicted by the wisdom of the Elders of the community for the crime of adult'ry. On'y the sentence remains. Elder?" Here, Cob nodded at Elder Oughta who came to stand before her, not looking at her.

"You understand your crime?"

She did not raise her head. Not even to look at the rope which had been strung over the branch of a nearby tree, or to watch Firoz being dragged there.

"You know which commandment you have violated? Which of God's laws you have trod upon so casually?"

Glory spit on the ground as close to him as she could manage.

"Number seven," said the Elder. "Thou shalt not commit adultery. Since the Pastor is not here to plead for you, there is only one punishment available to you. You know what that is?"

"Mr. Whitaker!" Rosa called. "He let us stay to *test* you! He's still *testing* you!"

The Elder frowned. A muscle in his shoulder twitched. He did not answer.

Something seemed to stir in Whitaker. He looked at Rosa as if he understood. He stepped forward, towards his father. "Is she right?" Whitaker asked him. "This ain't about Pastor at all? But about me? About whether I'm good enough to be your son?"

The Elder turned towards him. "First time you've challenged me in ten years," he replied. "And it's complete nonsense."

"No," Whitaker said, shaking his head slowly. "The kid's right! You're still testing, aren't you? Testing me. Still ashamed of who I was because of my spigger mom. And then you gave me Glory. To see...to see..." he faltered.

Elder's smile was tight. He turned away from Whitaker. "I gave you this whore because you couldn't have had anyone without me. And she's let you down, so I'm taking her away."

"No, I am," said Whitaker. And he held a rifle to his shoulder.

Only he aimed squarely at the Elder's head.

The roar of the torches suddenly became very loud in the silence that overcame the astonished townspeople. "Whitaker, *don't!*" admonished Glory from the steps. Through her arms were fastened tight, she implored him with a look of fear.

"That's okay," Whitaker said, looking up at her. "I'm sorry you and I never got to be friends again like when you was a kid in the woodshop. I would have liked you to be happy. If we set you free, maybe there's still a chance." There was a sharp retort, a rifle crack. Rosa wheeled her head, but the Elder had not moved. Hank, his gun to his eye, had taken a shot and the pitiful figure of Whitaker crumpled and fell to earth.

The Elder walked quickly over to his son and bent over his fallen figure. Elder Oughta's face grew lined and taut. His veiny hand touched the hair on his son's head.

He gave a curt nod and someone took Hank's gun. Two of the Elder's gorillas came up and took him by the arms. Hank in his ragged uniform looked surprised, as if he didn't understand, but he could not argue as the two gorillas took him into the woods.

Straightening up, the Elder turned his back on his son and gestured at two more of his gorillas. "Get my boy up. Take him away." They picked Whitaker up, and his body seemed somehow larger now, as though the dead weight of it filled the space.

A shot rang out from the woods, echoing off the distant hills.

The Elder's eyes were hard as he looked up at no one. Turning now once more towards Glory, he gestured with a finger.

"Wait!" cried Rosa. "Stop! You can't do this. They didn't do anything wrong!"

No one seemed to hear her. The townspeople were not shocked by her words. They barely registered them.

Firoz was being held by two men under the tree, his arms behind his back, the noose dropped around his neck. They would force him to watch Glory's stoning before they hung him.

Mrs. Bloodworthy stepped forward, moving towards Rosa. She held a rock in her hand, estimated its weight, but she never took her eyes off Rosa's own. At last she was right in front of the child.

"Mrs. Bloodworthy, don't!" pleaded Rosa.

For a few moments, the old woman held her gaze, and the rock. Then, at last, she seemed to make a decision. She dropped it, let it fall in front of Rosa's feet.

Rosa gave a sigh of relief. She swayed a little, putting her hand to her forehead. "That's good, Mrs. Bloodworthy," she said.

"Pick it up, baby," said Mrs. Bloodworthy.

Rosa's mouth opened, but she could not speak.

The old woman touched Rosa on the side of her head, then stroked her cheek.

Rosa tried to shake her face but her neck was frozen. Her mouth stayed open, locked in an expression of horror.

"Pick it up, child," Mrs. Bloodworthy repeated.

As she looked around, all the townspeople had stones in her hands and they were watching her. She saw the Elder's eyes on her from far away. Cob was in front of her, looming suddenly.

He handed her a stone. His eyes were rimmed with red as he looked at her, seeing ghosts in her face. "When the children were here, we always let them cast the first stone."

She looked at Glory who was weeping towards the ground, her feet bruised and scratched. Suddenly Rosa remembered the Pastor.

She turned to look into the darkness, but he was not visible beyond the torchlight. Had he gone, or was he still watching? Watching like everyone else, watching her, waiting to see if she would throw it?

The skin on Mrs. Bloodworthy's face grew tighter and she leaned in. "Rosa, dear, you've got to do this." The old woman's voice fell another level so that only Rosa could hear her, and she spoke more quickly, emphatic, enunciating every word. "I know it's difficult for you, it must seem cruel, but listen! You've got to throw that stone! When you do you'll be one of us." She looked quickly away, and then her eyes focused again on Rosa. "Please honey! If you don't, it won't be safe." She glanced quickly at Firoz, then darted her eyes away. "Don't you understand? You do, don't you? You've got to throw the stone!"

Rosa wanted to shake her head no. But she was overpowered by the weight of the rock, so heavy in her hand that she wanted only to be rid of it. And she felt gravity pulling Glory's weeping forehead towards the ground, and her own sight grew dark, until she couldn't see anything except where the stone would go.

A light burst into the space like the rays of a merciless sun and everything turned stark white. People covered their eyes as huge winds blew back their hair. The Elder limped a step or two away, shielding his face and looking up towards the bright deluge.

Figures jumped down from the sky, swinging down from the ends of ropes. Now there were twice as many people in the town square, half of them in sleek uniforms with sprayers in their hands. The townfolk tried to move out of the way, but there was nowhere to run. Those that tried to point their guns were immediately shot dead. From the edges of the circle, other Young Guns came in.

The Elder's gorillas tried to protect him, but they were easily outmatched by the overwhelming figures in the uniforms with their sprayer guns. One of those ran to Firoz and helped him off the steps and out of the noose.

Firoz was resisting. He was arguing, and Rosa thought he must be asking them to take Glory too. Instead, a man looked over at Rosa and came her way.

He grabbed at her arm. "No," she said, pulling away. "Mamma..."

Mrs. Bloodworthy panicked and pulled her other arm. "Let her go!" she cried. "She's our child. Our child!"

"No," Rosa said again. *"Wait!"* Her howl was lost in the terrible roar of the airship that still hovered overhead. She was attached to a rope that came from a mouth in the bottom of the ship, a mouth which was going to swallow her.

She screamed, she felt Mrs. Bloodworthy's fingers being pried away from her arm. As the rope went tight and she was snatched up into the air, she saw below people being escorted to different places by the Uniforms. Some were being taken into the ship, others towards the buildings, and still others to the woods.

When the ship finally closed its hole under her she decided she wanted to be in darkness for good.

Part Four - What Happened

But there was no darkness for her once the lights came on, not for a long time. She slept in a lit, locked room in a sterile bed while AVE's blared their commercials at her. Way back, before she had left Atlanta, the constant noise had been a comfort. Now she found she couldn't think straight with the noise.

The people who came to take care of her were nice, even though they couldn't cheer her up. There were so many dark faces. She had forgotten what she looked like.

She didn't know how long she had been there lying in bed with her face to the wall when a man shuffled in wearing a silk suit with a white blouse. She turned to look at him, his tired eyes, his mouth in the smallest approximation of a smile. After a minute of her staring, he guessed what the problem was.

"It's me. Firoz," he said to her in Spanish.

Her mouth dropped open. "Firoz, Naz!" she finally exclaimed. She hadn't spoken to anyone since she came here, and the name came out strangely, in an English accent. She tripped over her tongue as she tried to reshape the words. "Why do you look so good?"

But she knew the answer more quickly than she expected. She'd been processing the whole thing since they'd brought her in. Without realizing it, she'd put the pieces together and now she only needed him there to confirm the whole thing. "You were somebody important, weren't you?"

He nodded. "I was. I might still be. I don't know."

"You knew the Young Guns were coming," she said. No answer from Firoz. "Did you send for them?"

He shook his head. "Someone told them where I was. A boy, the one who turned me into an addict."

"Basil?"

"You know him?" The *Siyo* was astonished. Then he forgot the coincidence as he moved into a sideways reflection. "I would have been glad to die," he said. "Get that stone in the ---"

"Shut up, Firoz," Rosa interrupted. "Don't say that. Don't say it!" She covered her eyes with her hands to stop the image of those figures in the torchlight, waiting for her to throw.

She gave a shuddering breath. When it subsided, she managed to look through her fingers. "Where are we are now?"

"You haven't asked?" Firoz said, quite surprised.

"I haven't been able to talk," Rosa retorted. "I haven't done much but sleep for days. They put crap in my food to make me sleepy 'cause they don't want to talk to me."

"You're in a hospital in Atlanta Proper."

"Why would they take care of me?" Who the hell was she, a little nobody kid, being treated like some kind of political prisoner in this bland windowless place? Why hadn't they dumped her into some kind of home or left her on the street?

"I asked them to keep you here," Firoz said.

Rosa thought about that for a few seconds.

"Why would you do that?"

"You saved me...I thought if I could keep just one person alive—"

"I want to look for my parents," she interrupted.

"Your parents are dead," he replied.

Rosa sat still. Firoz, seeing that she would not respond, continued. "They got on a broken bus which limped to DC. They were arrested at the border for being in violation of a legal death warrant."

At last, hearing it, the truth of it, unquestionable, her eyes burned hard as if in a too-bright glare. She blinked, swallowed, and could not find her voice. Looking for the words to reply, the only one she could come up with was: "Why?" which she managed in a deep, husky voice. She shuddered and tried very, very hard to speak instead of sob: "Why did you kill them?"

"*I* didn't kill them!" he answered, looking wounded. "Not me! I was supposed to. But I didn't. I ran away."

Rosa was understanding less and less. "They weren't anybody important. Why would you be forced to kill my parents?"

"I was supposed to kill more than a million," Firoz clarified. "I ran so I wouldn't have to. I became an addict, and they were unable to give the order for a long time. Nobody wanted to take the responsibility."

Rosa wiped her nose and looked at Firoz. "How high up are you?"

"High," muttered Firoz. "High enough that my order to terminate more than a million people from the job-life rolls of the Corporate United States of America couldn't be taken by anyone else."

"But why did you have to give the order?"

Answering the question, Firoz's eyes clouded over. "It's just one tool in an infinitely complicated mechanism to prevent the collapse of the ecosystem and the economy. You see, a million die so that..."

He sounded like he would have gone on and on, and she couldn't bear to hear it. "Can I see their bodies?"

"Beg pardon?" said Firoz.

"Their *bodies!*" Rosa barked, feeling her face grow hot. "Their...corpses," she said, holding back the panic, the tears that would never stop once they started. "My parents."

"I..." Firoz began. Then he understood that she didn't want to know about the intricacies of his job. "I should have died, too," he said. "They're keeping me alive."

"What?" Rosa asked, with the tears beginning at last to make their way out. Firoz did not hand her a tissue. She started searching for one near the bed. That was when she saw the rose.

"After I left," he said, "They couldn't find anyone to take responsibility. Nobody wanted to terminate that many people. So they put my identity on someone, a cab driver or someone. They tried to get him to make the decision. They won't say where he is, but I think he's in prison, still serving my sentence."

They had left the rose for her. Sitting by the bed. A little worn, one petal broken off, otherwise intact.

"So now my identity is gone. I was Firoz Sattari, *Siyo* of the Noke Corporation. Now I'm nothing, not even a nobody. They don't know what to do with me. I guess they remember my talent, how good I was, so they're keeping me around until they can either put me back or they have no use for me."

"What about me?" Rosa wanted to know.

"I asked them to save you," Firoz went on, going back to his original monologue. "I thought at least that would make up for what I did."

Rosa realized she could not prevent this self-confessional. "What are you talking about?" she argued. "You didn't do anything but run."

"No," said Firoz slowly. "No, I did worse than that."

"You've been an addict stranded in a small town. What could you have done?"

Firoz gave her a level gaze. "Wherever I go, people die. Now that I've lived in Ascension, it can never be the same." He turned away. "CUSA intends to turn the entire area into a Young Guns base."

"So the town..."

"The town, like the woods that surround it, will be leveled. We'll probably be too close to Richmond and Bosses will argue, but CUSA will kill off the stupid ones and pay off the smart ones."

"What about all the people? Mrs. Bloodworthy? The Pastor and Glory and Cob..."

"I don't know," shrugged Firoz. "CUSA will buy some of them if they're useful. If they're not..." He let off.

Rosa wiped her eyes. She was too angry to cry in front of Firoz anymore. "Isn't there anything you can do?" she demanded.

"Me?"

"Yes, you, Mr. Big Shit *Siyo!*" she yelled. "Can't you save them? Don't you actually care about Glory?"

"Glory wanted an escape," Firoz said. "I don't think either of us cared how that happened."

Rosa could not answer that. She lay in bed, silent, for a long time. Firoz kept her company for a while, without saying anything more.

Rosa tried to turn over and go to sleep. Firoz wouldn't leave. After a few minutes she rolled back over and stared at him.

"Well?" she demanded.

"Well what?"

"What are we going to do?"

"We're going to watch," he said.

That took her by surprise. "Watch what?" she asked softly.

Firoz gestured at an AVE. Like a sunflower, it turned its sphere towards him. "Watch."

The AVE began expanding. Within its halo pictures of armies appeared, with interactive diagrams displaying their movements from the south and the north towards Virginia. It showed buildings being erected on a new site, and all the while the music played and played, selling candy and soft drinks and macaroni and cheese.

"Turn it off," Rosa said. "That makes me sick. Turn it off."

Firoz complied. The AVE winked like a forlorn eye, leaving the empty air in its place. But the images remained.

Rosa didn't say anything for a moment. She regarded Firoz, who was himself lost in thought. "I'm getting out of here," she said.

"You can't," Firoz replied.

"What do you mean?"

"They don't know what to do with you either. You can't just be on their books and not be reconciled. As long as you're here, you're anonymous. Once you leave, you're a dead person walking."

"I don't care about that," Rosa said. "I'd rather run for my life than be a zombie here. Isn't there a way to sneak me out, leave a door open, something?" Rosa said.

"Probably. But you have nowhere to go. Your parents are dead."

"Thanks for saying it again. Look, if you get me out the door, I can make my way."

"Then what?"

"What do you care?"

The addict, the *Siyo*, looked confused. But he nodded, uncomprehending. "I can get you out the door."

He had ensured her a surreptitious ride on a train through the forest, back to Buckhead. From there she went back to her old house, already occupied by some other family. That was fine. She didn't want to go in it anyway. But she found a bike to steal.

She pedaled through two downpours and the heat that came between them. At last she could ride no longer. She trudged along Glen Crest Road, her hospital shoes already beginning to wear out.

Now it came in sight at last. An old gray building set up against a graveyard.

The addicts were shambling from the front door. They had just been serviced. From somewhere a bell rang, the bell that sent them back out.

Rosa made her way to the front entrance, ignoring the blank looks of the sputtering men and women who brushed by her in the opposite direction, not listening to the comments they made either to her or about her. She only saw the Padre in black at the front of the pews, putting his things away.

When he saw her, his eyes closed halfway.

She got as close to him as she dared.

"Who are you?" he asked, quietly. "What do you want here?"

"I'm a friend of Basil's," she said.

He did not reply immediately. After a second's contemplation, "I remember you. What do you want?"

"I came to talk to Basil."

"He's gone," said the Padre.

"Where?"

"I can't say," shrugged the man in black, trying to look nonchalant. "He is old enough to make his way if he wants."

"So you got no apprentice," Rosa pointed out.

The man eyed her. "What's that to you?"

Rosa shuffled her feet. She had not been prepared to do this alone. But it didn't matter, because she knew what she wanted whether he would help her or not.

"I'm going to join," she said.

He looked surprised, then. "You can't be an addict," he said.

"No, I want to help you," she said. "To give the body and the blood."

He stared at her for a while, as if to try and figure out her game. "Why?" he wanted to know.

"Ain't got nothing else. Don't want to be nowhere else."

"What's your faith?"

"Raised *chuseno.*"

"Isn't that going to be a problem?"

"Not for me," she said, looking him in the eye. "What about you?"

The man cleared his throat. Clearly, he felt uncomfortable having the question put to him.

"Three days," he said at last, gruffly. "Three days you spend here, cleaning the bodily fluids of the faithful. We'll see how you like it."

She put her hands in her pockets. Something stabbed her. It was the wooden rose.

"Okay," said Rosa. "Okay."

The man nodded.

Turning her back on the pews she stepped forward to follow the man further into the church. Meanwhile the front door closed on the departing addicts. They vanished without a word into the hot mist, still waiting for the Body and the Blood to show them how to quit.

About the Author

A jazz musician who writes books, Adam Cole is the author of many works of speculative fiction including *Motherless Child* and *The Girl With the Bow*. He has been featured in Reader's Digest, Psychology Today and NBC.com and serves as a regular contributor to periodicals such as UpWorthy, Transzion and Fupping. He chronicles his journey through stage fright, self-improvement and the learning process in his popular blog series.

His journey has taken him through roles as a jazz musician, a music educator, and a choral director in public and private education. As co-director of the Grant Park Academy of the Arts, he advocates for the importance of the arts in education. He continues to take his many experiences in these fields and rework them into the worlds his dedicated readers have come to love.

Visit him at www.acole.net

CPSIA information can be obtained
at www.ICGtesting.com
Printed in the USA
BVHW081921280619
552238BV00001B/111/P